PENGUIN CLASSICS

Maigret and the Old People

'Extraordinary masterpieces of the twentieth century'
– John Banville

'A brilliant writer'
– India Knight

'Intense atmosphere and resonant detail . . . make Simenon's fiction remarkably like life'
– Julian Barnes

'A truly wonderful writer . . . marvellously readable – lucid, simple, absolutely in tune with the world he creates'
– Muriel Spark

'Few writers have ever conveyed with such a sure touch, the bleakness of human life'
– A. N. Wilson

'Compelling, remorseless, brilliant'
– John Gray

'A writer of genius, one whose simplicity of language creates indelible images that the florid stylists of our own day can only dream of'
– *Daily Mail*

'The mysteries of the human personality are revealed in all their disconcerting complexity'
– Anita Brookner

'One of the greatest writers of our time'
– *The Sunday Times*

'I love reading Simenon. He makes me think of Chekhov'
– William Faulkner

'One of the great psychological novelists of this century'
– *Independent*

'The greatest of all, the most genuine novelist we have had in literature'
– André Gide

'Simenon ought to be spoken of in the same breath as Camus, Beckett and Kafka'
– *Independent on Sunday*

GEORGES SIMENON

Maigret and the Old People

Translated by SHAUN WHITESIDE

PENGUIN BOOKS

PENGUIN CLASSICS

UK | USA | Canada | Ireland | Australia
India | New Zealand | South Africa

Penguin Books is part of the Penguin Random House group of companies
whose addresses can be found at global.penguinrandomhouse.com.

First published in French as *Maigret et les Vieillards* by Presses de le Cité 1960
This translation first published 2018

005

Copyright © Georges Simenon Limited, 1960
Translation copyright © Shaun Whiteside, 2018
GEORGES SIMENON ® Simenon.tm
MAIGRET ® Georges Simenon Limited
All rights reserved

The moral rights of the author and translator have been asserted

Set in 12.5/15 pt Dante MT Std
Typeset by Jouve (UK), Milton Keynes
Printed and bound in Great Britain by Clays Ltd, Elcograf S.p.A.

ISBN: 978-0-241-30389-4

www.greenpenguin.co.uk

Maigret and the Old People

1.

It was one of those exceptional months of May, the kind you only encounter two or three times in your life, and which have the luminosity, the taste, the smell of childhood memories. Maigret called it a 'May of hymns', because it reminded him both of his first communion and his first spring in Paris, when everything was still new and wonderful to him.

In the street, on the bus, in his office, he was often pulled up short, struck by a far-away sound, by a warm breeze, by the bright patch of a blouse that carried him back twenty or thirty years.

The day before, when they were about to go to dinner with the Pardons, his wife had asked him, almost blushing:

'Don't I look too silly in a floral dress, at my age?'

That evening their friends the Pardons had introduced a novelty. Rather than inviting them to their house, they had taken the Maigrets to a little restaurant on Boulevard du Montparnasse, where the four of them had dined outside.

Maigret and his wife, without a word, had exchanged knowing glances, because it was outside this very restaurant, thirty years before, that they had enjoyed their first meal together.

'Do they have mutton stew?'

The restaurant had changed owners, but there was still mutton stew on the menu, wobbly lamps on the tables, potted plants in tubs and Chavignol by the carafe.

All four of them were very cheerful. At the café, Pardon had taken from his pocket a journal with a white cover.

'By the way, Maigret, they're talking about you in the *Lancet*.'

Maigret, who knew the name of the famous and very austere English medical journal, had frowned.

'I mean that they're talking about your profession in general. The article is by one Dr Richard Fox, and I will translate the passage that will interest you more or less literally:

'"A skilful psychiatrist, based on his scientific knowledge and surgical experience, is quite well placed to understand human beings. But it is possible, particularly if he is influenced by theory, that he will understand them less well than an exceptional schoolteacher, than a novelist, or even a policeman."'

They had discussed this for a while, sometimes joking, sometimes in a more serious tone. Then the Maigrets had walked together along silent streets.

Maigret was not yet aware that the London doctor's words would come to mind several times over the next few days, or that the memories stirred in him by this perfect month of May would come to seem almost like a premonition.

The very next day, on the bus that took him towards Châtelet, he found himself looking at faces with the same curiosity as when he had just arrived in the capital.

And it seemed strange to him to be climbing the stairs of the Police Judiciaire as detective chief inspector and receiving respectful greetings on the way. Was it really such a long time since he had first stepped, awestruck, into this building where the police chiefs still seemed like figures of legend to him?

He felt both light and melancholy. With the window open, he went through his mail and called in young Lapointe to give him instructions.

In twenty-five years, the Seine hadn't changed, and neither had the passing boats, or the anglers who were still in the same spot as if they hadn't moved from it.

Taking little puffs on his pipe, he did his housework, as he called it, ridding the office of the files that were piled up there, clearing up unimportant matters, when the telephone rang.

'Can you come and see me for a moment, Maigret?' the commissioner asked.

Without hurrying, Maigret made towards the chief's office and went and stood by the window.

'I have just had a strange phone call from Quai d'Orsay. Not from the foreign minister in person, but from his cabinet chief. I'm being asked to send someone down there as a matter of urgency, someone capable of taking responsibility. Those are the words they used.

'"An inspector?" I asked.

'"It would be better if it was someone more important. It's probably a crime."'

The two men looked at each other with a hint of mischief in their eyes, because neither of them was fond of ministries, let alone one as stuffy as the Ministry of Foreign Affairs.

'I thought you would want to go there yourself . . .'

'Perhaps that would be better . . .'

The commissioner picked up a piece of paper from his desk and held it out to Maigret.

'You'll have to ask for a certain Monsieur Cromières. He's waiting for you.'

'Is he the cabinet chief?'

'No. He's the person who is dealing with the matter.'

'Should I take an inspector with me?'

'I know nothing more than what I have just told you. These people like to be mysterious.'

Maigret took Janvier along in the end, and they both took a taxi. At Quai d'Orsay they weren't directed towards the main staircase but, at the end of the courtyard, towards a narrow and rather uninviting staircase, as if they were being ushered through the wings at a theatre or the service entrance of a restaurant. They wandered along the corridors for a while before finding a waiting room, and a liveried bailiff, indifferent to Maigret's name, made him fill in a form.

At last they were led into an office, where a functionary, very young and immaculately dressed, was standing still and silent, facing an old woman as impassive as himself. It looked as if they had been waiting like that for a long time, probably since the phone call from Quai d'Orsay to the Police Judiciaire.

'Detective Chief Inspector Maigret?'

Maigret introduced Janvier, whom the young man barely deigned to glance at.

'Since I don't know what the matter is, I asked one of my inspectors to come along just in case . . .'

'Take a seat.'

Cromières liked above all to give himself important airs, and there was a very condescending 'Foreign Affairs' tone in his way of speaking.

'If the ministry directly approached the Police Judiciaire . . .'

He uttered the word 'ministry' as if it were a sacrosanct institution.

'. . . it is because, inspector, we find ourselves in the presence of a highly unusual case . . .'

While observing him, Maigret also observed the old woman, who must have been deaf in one ear, because she craned her neck to hear better, her head lowered, focusing her attention to the movement of the man's lips.

'Mademoiselle . . .'

Cromières consulted a file on his desk.

'Mademoiselle Larrieu is the maidservant, or rather the housekeeper, of one of our most distinguished former ambassadors, the Count of Saint-Hilaire, who I am sure you have heard of . . .'

Maigret remembered the name from reading it in the papers, but it seemed to go back to a time long past.

'Since his retirement, about a dozen years ago, the Count of Saint-Hilaire has lived in Paris, in his apartment on Rue Saint-Dominique. Mademoiselle Larrieu appeared here at half past eight this morning, and had to wait for a while before being received by a suitably senior official.'

Maigret imagined the empty offices at half past eight

in the morning, the motionless old woman in the waiting room, her eyes fixed on the door.

'Mademoiselle Larrieu has worked for the Count of Saint-Hilaire for over forty years.'

'Forty-six,' she corrected him.

'Forty-six, then. She followed him to different postings and looked after his house. For the last twelve years she has lived alone with the ambassador in his apartment on Rue Saint-Dominique. It's there that, this morning, after finding the bedroom empty when she brought her employer his breakfast, she found him dead in his office.'

The old woman looked at each of them in turn, her eyes keen, searching and suspicious.

'According to her, Saint-Hilaire had been shot by one bullet or several.'

'She didn't go to the police?'

The fair-haired young man assumed a smug look.

'I understand your surprise. Don't forget that Mademoiselle Larrieu has lived much of her life in the diplomatic milieu. While the count may no longer have been active, she still felt that a certain discretion was required . . .'

Maigret glanced at Janvier.

'And it didn't occur to her to call a doctor?'

'Apparently the death leaves no doubt.'

'Who is at Rue Saint-Dominique at the moment?'

'No one. Mademoiselle Larrieu came straight here. To avoid any misunderstandings or wasted time, I am authorized to affirm that the Count of Saint-Hilaire was not in possession of any state secrets, and that we should not seek a political cause for his death. Extreme caution is also indispensable. When a case concerns a prominent man, particularly one who worked for the Foreign Ministry, the newspapers tend all too often to puff these stories and come up with the most unlikely hypotheses . . .'

The young man got to his feet.

'Might I suggest that we go there now?'

'You too?' Maigret asked innocently.

'Don't worry. I have no intention of interfering in your inquiry. If I come with you it is only to make sure that there is nothing at the scene that might cause us embarrassment.'

The old woman had stood up as well. All four of them went down the stairs.

'It will be better to take a taxi. It will be more discreet than a ministry limousine . . .'

The journey was ridiculously short. The car stopped outside an imposing late eighteenth-century house with no crowd, no onlookers in front of it. Beneath the arch, once they had passed through the coach-gate, it was cool, and they could see, in what looked more like a drawing room than a lodge, a concierge in a uniform as imposing as the one worn by the bailiff at the ministry.

They climbed four steps to the left. The lift was motionless, in a dark marble hall. The old woman took a key from her bag and opened a walnut door.

'This way . . .'

She led them along a corridor to a room that must have overlooked the courtyard, but whose shutters and curtains were closed. It was Mademoiselle Larrieu who turned on the electric switch, and, at the foot of a mahogany table, they saw a body lying on the red carpet.

The three men took off their hats with the same movement, while the old maidservant looked at them with a kind of challenge.

'What did I tell you?' she seemed to be muttering.

There was no need to lean over the body, in fact, to know that the Count of Saint-Hilaire was well and truly dead. A bullet had entered the right eye, exploding the skull, and, judging by the rips in the black velvet dressing gown and the bloodstains, other bullets had struck the body in several places.

Monsieur Cromières was the first to approach the desk.

'You see. Apparently he was busy correcting proofs . . .'

'He was writing a book?'

'His memoirs. Two volumes have already been published. It would be ridiculous to see that as the cause of his death, because Saint-Hilaire was the most discreet of men, and his memoirs were literary and artistic in style, rather than political.'

Cromières used flowery language and liked the sound of his own voice, and Maigret was starting to get irritated. There they were, the four of them, in a room with closed shutters, at ten o'clock in the morning, while the sun was shining outside, looking at a twisted and bloody old man.

'I suppose,' the inspector growled, not without irony, 'that we still need to involve the prosecutor's office?'

There was a telephone on the desk, but he preferred not to touch it.

'Janvier, go and call from the lodge. Alert the prosecutor's office and the local chief inspector . . .'

The old woman looked at them one after the other as if she had been given the job of keeping an eye on them. Her eyes were hard, without sympathy or human warmth.

'What are you doing?' Maigret said as he saw the man from the ministry opening the doors of a bookshelf.

'I'm taking a look . . .'

He added with a confidence disagreeable in one so young:

'It is my role to check, just in case, that there are no papers here whose disclosure might be inopportune . . .'

Was he as young as he looked? Which service did he actually belong to? Without waiting for the inspector's assent, he studied the contents of the library, opening files which he put back in place one after another.

Meanwhile, Maigret paced back and forth, impatient and ill-humoured.

Cromières attacked the other furniture, the drawers, and the old woman was still standing near the door, her hat on her head and handbag in her hand.

'Would you take me to his bedroom?'

She walked ahead of the man from the ministry, while Maigret stayed in the office, where Janvier joined him soon afterwards.

'Where are they?'

'In the bedroom . . .'

'What are we doing?'

'Nothing for now. I'm waiting for this gentleman to be so kind as to make room for us.'

He wasn't the only thing that was irritating Maigret. It was also the way in which the case was presented and, perhaps more than anything, the unfamiliar world in which he found himself suddenly immersed.

'The chief inspector will be here in a moment.'

'Have you told him what it's about?'

'I just asked him to bring the pathologist.'

'Did you phone Criminal Records?'

'Moers is on the way with his men.'

'And the prosecutor's office?'

'They're on their way too.'

The office was spacious and comfortable. While there was nothing solemn about it, it did have a certain refinement that had struck the inspector as soon as he walked in. Every piece of furniture, every object was beautiful in itself. And the old man on the ground, with the top of his head almost blown away, maintained quite a handsome appearance in this context.

Cromières came back, followed by the old housekeeper.

'I don't think there's anything more to be done here. Once again, I recommend prudence and discretion. It cannot be a suicide, since there is no weapon in the room. Are we agreed on that? I will leave you to discover whether anything has been stolen. In any case, it would be unpleasant if the press were to make a lot of noise about this business . . .'

Maigret looked at him in silence.

'I will telephone you, if you like, to see if there are any fresh developments,' the young man went on. 'It may well be that you need some information, and you can always come to me.'

'Thank you.'

'In a chest of drawers in the bedroom you will even find a certain number of letters which will probably surprise you. It's an old story that everyone at the ministry knows and which has nothing to do with today's tragedy.'

He was plainly leaving reluctantly.

'I'm relying on you . . .'

Old Mademoiselle Larrieu followed him to see him out the door, and she appeared again a little later with neither her hat nor her handbag. She had come not to put herself at the inspector's service, but to keep an eye on the two men.

'Do you sleep in the apartment?'

When Maigret addressed her, she wasn't looking at him and seemed not to have heard. He repeated his question, more loudly. This time she lowered her head and stretched her good ear towards him.

'Yes. I have a little room behind the kitchen.'

'Are there any other servants?'

'Not here, no.'

'You do the housework and the cooking?'

'Yes.'

'How old are you?'

'Seventy-three.'

'And the Count of Saint-Hilaire?'

'Seventy-seven.'

'At what time did you leave him last night?'

'At about ten o'clock.'

'Was he in this office?'

'Yes.'

'Was he waiting for anybody?'

'He didn't tell me.'

'Did he sometimes have people over for dinner?'

'His nephew.'

'Where does his nephew live?'

'On Rue Jacob. He's an antiques dealer.'

'Is he called Saint-Hilaire as well?'

'No. He's the son of the count's sister. His name is Mazeron.'

'Have you got that, Janvier?

'This morning, when you found the body . . . Because it was this morning when you found him, wasn't it?'

'Yes. At eight o'clock.'

'You didn't think of telephoning Monsieur Mazeron?'

'No.'

'Why not?'

She didn't reply. She had the staring eye of certain birds and, also like certain birds, she sometimes perched on one leg.

'Don't you like him?'

'Who?'

'Monsieur Mazeron?'

'It has nothing to do with me.'

Maigret now knew that she was going to be far from easy.

'What has nothing to do with you?'

'The family's business.'

'The nephew didn't get on with his uncle?'

'I didn't say that.'

'Did they get on well?'

'I don't know.'

'What were you doing yesterday, at ten o'clock in the evening?'

'I went to bed.'

'At what time did you get up?'

'At six o'clock, as usual.'

'And you didn't set foot in this room?'

'I had no business there.'

'The door was closed?'

'If it had been open, I would have noticed straight away that something had happened.'

'Why?'

'Because the lamps were still lit.'

'As they are now?'

'No. The ceiling lamp wasn't lit. Only the lamp on the desk and the standard lamp in that corner.'

'What did you do, at six o'clock?'

'I washed myself, first of all.'

'And then?'

'I cleaned my kitchen and went to buy croissants.'

'And the apartment stayed empty during that time?'

'Like every morning.'

'And then?'

'I made some coffee, I had something to eat, and finally I took the tray to the bedroom.'

'Was the bed unmade?'

'No.'

'Was the place untidy?'

'No.'

'Last night, when you left him, was the count wearing that black dressing gown?'

'As he did every evening when he didn't go out.'

'Did he go out often?'

'He liked the cinema.'

'Did he have friends for dinner?'

'Hardly ever. From time to time he went to have lunch in town.'

'Do you know the names of the people he met?'

'It's none of my business.'

The doorbell rang. It was the district chief inspector, accompanied by his secretary. He looked at the desk in surprise, then at the old woman, and at last at Maigret, whose hand he shook.

'How come you got here before us? Was she the one who called you?'

'Not at all. She went to Quai d'Orsay. Do you know the victim?'

'He's the former ambassador, isn't he? I know him by name and by sight. He used to take a walk in the neighbourhood every morning. Who did it?'

'We don't know anything yet. I'm waiting for the prosecutor's office.'

'The registrar doctor will be here very shortly.'

No one touched the furniture or the ornaments. There was a curious atmosphere of unease, and it was a relief when the doctor arrived; he gave a little whistle when he bent over the body.

'I don't suppose I can turn him over before the photographers arrive?'

'Don't touch him . . . Do you have an approximate idea of the time of death?'

'A while ago . . . At first sight, I would say about ten hours . . . It's strange . . .'

'What's strange?'

'He seems to have been hit by at least four bullets . . . One here . . . Another one there . . .'

Kneeling, he examined the body more closely.

'I don't know what the pathologist will think. For my part, I wouldn't be surprised if the first bullet killed him outright, and they went on shooting anyway. Bear in mind that this is only a hypothesis . . .'

In less than five minutes the apartment filled up. First the prosecutor's office, represented by the deputy, Pasquier, and an examining magistrate, whom Maigret did not know well, and whose name was Urbain de Chézaud.

Dr Paul's successor, Dr Tudelle, came with them. Immediately after came the invasion of Criminal Records, with their cumbersome equipment.

'Who found the body?'

'The housekeeper.'

Maigret pointed at the old woman, who, with no apparent emotion, continued to keep a close eye on what everyone was up to.

'Have you questioned her?'

'Not yet. I've just exchanged a few words with her.'

'Does she know anything?'

'If she does, it won't be easy to make her speak.'

He told him the story of the foreign minister.

'Has anything been stolen?'

'Not at first sight. I'm waiting for Criminal Records to finish their work and tell me.'

'Family?'

'A nephew.'

'Has he been told?'

'Not yet. I plan to go and inform him myself while my men are working. He lives not far from here, on Rue Jacob.'

Maigret could have called the antiques dealer to ask him to come, but he preferred to meet him in his own setting.

'If you don't need me, I'll go there right now. Janvier, you stay here . . .'

It was a great relief to see daylight again, the patches of sunlight beneath the trees on Boulevard Saint-Germain. The air was mild, the women dressed in light colours, and a council water-cart was slowly moistening the middle of the carriageway.

He found the shop on Rue Jacob without any difficulty, its windows containing only old weapons, particularly swords. He pushed open the door, making a bell ring, and stood there for two or three minutes before a man emerged from the darkness.

Because his uncle was seventy-seven, Maigret wouldn't have expected the nephew to be a young man. He was nonetheless surprised that the man standing in front of him looked quite old.

'Can I help you?'

He had a long, pale face with bristling eyebrows; his head was almost bald and his floating clothes made him look thinner than he was.

'Are you Monsieur Mazeron?'

'Alain Mazeron, that's right.'

The shop was crammed with other weapons: mus-
kets, blunderbusses and, right at the back, two suits of
armour.

'Detective Chief Inspector Maigret, Police Judiciaire.'

The man frowned. Mazeron was trying to understand.

'You are the nephew of the Count of Saint-Hilaire, isn't
that right?'

'He's my uncle, yes. Why?'

'When did you last see him?'

He replied without hesitation:

'The day before yesterday.'

'Do you have a family?'

'I'm married with children.'

'When you saw your uncle the day before yesterday,
did he seem to be in his normal state?'

'Yes. He was even quite cheerful. Why are you asking
me that question?'

'Because he's dead.'

Maigret saw the same suspicion in the man's eyes as he
had in the old housekeeper.

'Has there been an accident?'

'In a sense . . .'

'What do you mean?'

'That he was killed last night, in his office, by several
bullets fired from a revolver or an automatic pistol.'

The antique dealer's face filled with disbelief.

'Do you know if he had any enemies?'

'No . . . Certainly not . . .'

If Mazeron had just said no, Maigret wouldn't have paid

attention. The 'certainly not' sounded a little like a corrective and made him prick up his ears.

'You have no idea who might have an interest in your uncle's death?'

'No . . . No one . . .'

'Was he very wealthy?'

'He had a little money . . . He lived mostly off his pension . . .'

'Did he sometimes come here?'

'Sometimes . . .'

'To have lunch or dinner with the family?'

Mazeron seemed distracted and replied through pursed lips as if thinking about something else.

'No . . . More in the morning, when he took his walk . . .'

'He came in to chat with you . . . ?'

'That's right. He came in, sat down for a moment . . .'

'Did you go and see him at his flat?'

'From time to time . . .'

'With your family?'

'No . . .'

'You have children, you told me?'

'Two! Two daughters . . .'

'And you live in this building?'

'On the first floor . . . One of my daughters, the elder one, is in England . . . The second, Marcelle, lives with her mother . . .'

'You don't live with your wife?'

'Not for some years . . .'

'Are you divorced?'

'No . . . It's complicated . . . Do you think we should go to my uncle's?'

He went and fetched his hat from the semi-darkness of the back of the shop, hung a sign on the door saying he would be back soon, locked it and followed Maigret along the pavement.

'Do you know what happened?' he asked.

He sounded concerned and worried.

'I know hardly anything.'

'Has anything been stolen?'

'I don't think so. There was no sign of disorder in the flat.'

'What does Jaquette say?'

'You mean the housekeeper?'

'Yes. That's her name . . . I don't know if that's her real name, but we've always called her Jaquette . . .'

'Do you like her?'

'Why do you ask me that?'

'She doesn't seem to like you.'

'She doesn't like anyone but my uncle. If it had been up to her, no one would ever have stepped inside the flat.'

'Do you think she would have been capable of killing him?'

Mazeron looked at him in astonishment.

'Her, kill him?'

It clearly struck him as the most ridiculous idea. And yet after a moment he caught himself considering it.

'No! It's not possible . . .'

'You hesitated.'

'Because of her jealousy . . .'

'You mean that she loved him?'

'She hasn't always been an old woman . . .'

'You think there might have been something between them?'

'It's quite likely. I wouldn't dare to swear to it. With a man like my uncle it's hard to know . . . Have you seen any photographs of Jaquette when she was young?'

'I haven't seen anything yet.'

'You will . . . It's all very complicated. Particularly that it's all happening right now . . .'

'What do you mean by that?'

Alain Mazeron looked at Maigret with a kind of weariness and sighed:

'Essentially, I see that you don't know anything.'

'What should I know?'

'I wonder . . . It's an annoying business . . . Have you found the letters?'

'I'm just starting my investigation.'

'It's Wednesday, isn't it?'

Maigret nodded.

'The day of the funeral . . .'

'Whose funeral?'

'The Prince of V—. You'll understand when you've read the letters . . .'

Just as they reached Rue Saint-Dominique, the Criminal Records car set off, and Moers waved at Maigret.

2.

'What are you thinking about, chief?'

Janvier was surprised by the effect of the question, which he had asked only to break quite a long silence. It seemed as if the words didn't immediately reach Maigret's brain, as if they were only sounds that he needed to re-arrange in order to untangle their meaning.

The inspector looked at his companion with big vague eyes and an embarrassed expression, as if he had just acci-dentally revealed one of his secrets.

'About those people . . .' he murmured.

Obviously he wasn't talking about the ones lunching around them in this restaurant on Rue de Bourgogne, but other ones, the ones they had never heard of the day before, while today their task was to discover their secret lives.

Every time he bought a suit, an overcoat, a pair of shoes, Maigret wore them first in the evening, when walking with his wife in the streets of the neighbourhood or to go to the cinema.

'I need to get used to them . . .' he would say to Madame Maigret, who mocked him affectionately.

It was the same when he immersed himself into a new investigation. The others didn't notice, because of his mas-sive bulk and the calm expression on his face, which they took for confidence. In fact, he passed through a more or less lengthy period of hesitation, unease, even timidity.

He had to get used to an unfamiliar context, a house, a way of life, people who had their habits, their ways of thinking and expressing themselves.

With some categories of people it was relatively simple, for example with the more or less regular clients or those who resembled them.

With the others, he had to learn everything all over again, particularly given his suspicion of rules and ready-made ideas.

In this case he had an additional handicap. This morning he had established contact with a milieu which was not only relatively closed but on which his childhood memories cast a particular light.

He realized that in all the time he had spent at Rue Saint-Dominique he had not shown his usual ease; he had been awkward; his questions were reticent and clumsy. Had Janvier noticed?

If he had, it certainly wouldn't have occurred to Janvier that it had something to do with Maigret's distant past, the years spent in the shadow of a chateau where his father was the estate manager, and where for a long time the Count and Countess of Saint-Fiacre had seemed to him like creatures of a unique species.

The two men had chosen this restaurant on Rue de Bourgogne for their lunch because they were able to sit outside, and they had quickly noticed that the establishment was frequented by civil servants from the surrounding ministries, particularly the Office of the

President, it seemed, with some officers in civilian clothes who belonged to the War Ministry.

They were not just any old clerks. They all had at least the rank of chief clerk, and Maigret was surprised to see that they were so young. He was also surprised by their confidence. Judging by their way of speaking and behaving, they seemed to be sure of themselves. Since some of them had recognized him and were talking about him under their breath, he was irritated by their knowing looks and ironic manner.

Did the people on Quai des Orfèvres, who were also civil servants, give the same impression of having answers to every question?

That was what he was thinking about at the moment when Janvier had drawn him from his daydream. About that morning in Rue Saint-Dominique. About the dead man, Count Armand de Saint-Hilaire, a long-time ambassador, who had just been murdered at the age of seventy-seven. About the strange Jaquette Larrieu and her little staring eyes that penetrated to his core as she listened to him, her head tilted, attentively watching the movement of his lips. About Alain Mazeron, last of all, pale and soft, lonely in his shop on Rue Jacob, among the swords and the armour, whom Maigret found himself unable to categorize.

What were the terms used by the English doctor in the article in the *Lancet*? He couldn't remember. By and large, they meant that an exceptional schoolteacher, a novelist or a policeman are better placed than a doctor or a psychiatrist to penetrate the depths of the human mind.

Why did the policeman come last, after the schoolteacher and above all the novelist?

He was slightly perplexed by that. As if to prove the author of the article wrong, he was keen to find his bearings in this new case.

They had started with asparagus and were now being served skate in black butter. The sky over the street was still as blue as before, and the passing women wore light-coloured dresses.

Before deciding to go and have lunch, Maigret and Janvier had spent an hour and a half in the flat of the dead man, which was already becoming more familiar to them.

The body had been taken to the Forensic Institute, where Dr Tudelle was doing the post-mortem. The people from the prosecutor's office and Criminal Records had gone. With a sigh of relief Maigret had opened curtains and shutters to let the sunlight into the rooms, giving the furniture and the ornaments their normal everyday appearance.

The inspector was not troubled by the fact that old Jaquette and the nephew followed in his wake, keeping a close eye on his movements and facial expressions, and from time to time he turned towards them to ask them a question.

They had probably been surprised to see him moving around for so long without looking at anything in particular, as if viewing a property that he planned to rent.

He was very interested in the office, so stuffy in the morning in artificial light, and he kept returning to it with a secret pleasure, because it was one of the most agreeable rooms he had ever seen.

The room had a high ceiling and was lit by French

windows that opened on to a flight of three steps, beyond which one discovered, not without surprise, a well-kept lawn, a huge lime tree standing in a world of stone.

'Who has access to this garden?' he had asked, looking up at the windows of other apartments.

The answer came from Mazeron:

'My uncle.'

'No other tenants?'

'No. The building belonged to him. He was born here. His father, who still had a considerable fortune, occupied the ground floor and the floor above. When he died, my uncle, who had already lost his mother, kept this little flat and the garden.'

This simple detail was significant. Was it not rare, in Paris, for a seventy-seven-year-old man to go on living in the house of his birth?

'And when he was an ambassador abroad?'

'He closed the apartment and came back for his holidays. Contrary to what one might imagine, the building brought him hardly any income. Most of the tenants have been here for so long that they pay derisory rents, and some years, with repairs and taxes, my uncle was out of pocket.'

There were not many rooms. The office stood in for the drawing room. Beside it there was a dining room, opposite the kitchen and a bedroom and a bathroom that looked out on to the street.

'Where do you sleep?' Maigret had asked Jaquette.

She had asked him to repeat the question, and he had started thinking that this must be an odd habit of hers.

'Behind the kitchen.'

There, he had found a kind of box room with an iron bed, a wardrobe and a basin with running water. A large ebony crucifix was fixed above a stoup decorated with a sprig of box-tree leaves.

'Was the Count of Saint-Hilaire religious?'

'He never missed Sunday mass, even when he was in Russia.'

The most striking thing was a subtle harmony, a refinement that Maigret would have had difficulty defining. The furniture was in different styles, and no one had taken the trouble to try to make it match. Even so, each room had its own beauty, each one had acquired the same patina, the same personality.

The walls of the office were entirely covered with bound books, while others, with white or yellow covers, were lined up on the shelves in the corridor.

'Was the window closed when you found the body?'

'You were the one who opened it. I haven't even touched the curtains.'

'And the bedroom window?'

'It was closed as well. The count felt the cold.'

'Who had the key to the apartment?'

'He and I both had one, no one else.'

Janvier had questioned the concierge. The little door cut into the monumental coach-gate was left open until midnight. The concierge never went to bed before that time; however, he sometimes sat in his bedroom behind the lodge, from where he couldn't necessarily see the people going in and out.

The previous day he hadn't noticed anything unusual. The house was calm, he kept insistently repeating. He had been there for thirty years, and the police had never had cause to set foot in the building.

It was too soon to reconstruct what had happened the previous evening. They would have to wait for the report from the pathologist, then the one from Moers and his men.

One thing seemed obvious: Saint-Hilaire hadn't gone to bed. He was wearing dark-grey trousers with fine stripes, a slightly starched white shirt, a polka-dotted bow tie and, as usual when he stayed at home, he had put on his black velvet dressing gown.

'Did he sometimes stay up late?'

'It depends what you mean by "late".'

'What time did he go to bed?'

'I almost always went to bed before him.'

It was exasperating. The most banal questions were met with a wall of suspicion; the old maidservant seldom gave a direct response.

'You didn't hear him leaving his office?'

'Go to my bedroom and you will notice that you can't hear anything but the noise of the lift on the other side of the wall.'

'How did he spend his evenings?'

'Reading. Writing. Correcting the proofs of his book.'

'Did he go to bed at around midnight, for example?'

'Perhaps shortly before, or shortly afterwards, depending on the day.'

'And then did he sometimes call you, needing your services?'

'To do what?'

'He might have wanted a herbal tea before going to bed, or . . .'

'He never drank herbal tea. And besides, he had his drinks cabinet . . .'

'What did he drink?'

'Wine with meals, claret. A glass of cognac in the evening . . .'

They had found the empty glass on the desk, and the specialists from Criminal Records had taken it away to check it for fingerprints.

If the old man had had a visitor, he didn't seem to have offered them anything to drink, because they couldn't find another glass in the office.

'Did the count own a firearm?'

'Hunting rifles. They're stored in the cupboard at the end of the corridor.'

'Did he hunt?'

'Sometimes, when he was invited to a chateau.'

'Did he have a pistol or a revolver?'

She had dug her heels in again, and when she did this her pupils shrank like a cat's, her face became frozen and blank.

'Did you hear my question?'

'What did you ask me?'

Maigret repeated his words.

'I think he had a revolver.'

'With a cylinder?'

'What do you mean by "cylinder"?'

He had tried to explain. No. It wasn't a gun with a cylinder. It was a flat gun, bluish, with a short barrel.

'Where did he keep this automatic?'

'I don't know. I haven't seen it for ages. The last time, it was in the chest of drawers.'

'In his bedroom?'

She had gone and shown him the drawer in question, which contained only handkerchiefs, sock suspenders and braces in different colours. The other drawers were full of carefully folded linen, shirts, underpants, handkerchiefs and, right at the bottom, the items that went with dinner jackets and tails.

'When did you last see the automatic?'

'Years ago.'

'Approximately how many?'

'I don't know. Time passes so quickly . . .'

'And you never saw it anywhere except in the chest of drawers?'

'No. Perhaps he put it in a drawer in his office. I never opened those drawers, and in any case they were always locked.'

'You didn't know why?'

'Why do people lock items of furniture?'

'He wasn't suspicious of you?'

'I'm sure he wasn't.'

'Of whom, then?'

'Don't you lock any of your furniture?'

There was a key, in fact, a very ornate bronze key, which opened the drawers of the Empire desk. The contents hadn't revealed anything, except that Saint-Iilaire, like everyone else, accumulated tiny useless objects, such as old empty wallets, two or three cigar-holders in gold-ringed amber which no one had used for a long time, a cigar-cutter, some drawing pins, some paper-clips, pencils and propelling pencils in all colours.

Another drawer had contained the writing paper marked with a crown, envelopes, visiting cards and carefully rolled-up bits of thread, glue, a penknife with a broken blade.

The copper-latticed doors of one bookcase were lined with green fabric. Inside, there were no books, but on all the shelves there were bundles of letters carefully tied with thread, each bundle bearing a dated label.

'Is this what you were referring to just now?' Maigret had asked Alain Mazeron.

The nephew had nodded his head.

'Do you know who these letters are from?'

He had nodded again.

'Was it your uncle who told you about them?'

'I can't remember if he told me, but everyone knows about them.'

'What do you mean by "everyone"?'

'In the world of diplomacy, in elevated circles.'

'Have you read any of these letters?'

'Never.'

'You may leave us and go and make lunch,' Maigret said to Jaquette.

'You think I'm going to eat on a day like this!'

'Leave us anyway. I'm sure you'll find something to do.'

She was obviously horrified at the idea of leaving him alone with the nephew. Several times he had caught the almost hate-filled glances that she darted at him on the sly.

'Did you hear me?'

'I know it's not my business, but . . .'

'What?'

'A person's letters are sacred . . .'

'Even if they might help us find a murderer?'

'They won't help you do anything at all.'

'I'll probably need you shortly. In the meantime . . .'

He had looked at the door, and Jaquette had left reluctantly. Wouldn't she have been indignant if she had been able to see Maigret taking the place of the Count of Saint-Hilaire at the desk on which Janvier was lining up the piles of letters?

'Take a seat,' he had said to Mazeron. 'Do you know who this correspondence is from?'

'Yes. I'm sure you'll see that all of these letters are signed Isi.'

'Who is Isi?'

'Isabelle of V—. Princess of V—. My uncle always called her Isi.'

'Was she his mistress?'

Why did Maigret think the man had the face of a sexton, as if sextons had to have a particular physique? Mazeron too, like Jaquette, had let a certain amount of time pass before answering the questions.

'Apparently they weren't lovers.'

Maigret had untied the thread of a bundle of yellowing letters dating from 1914, a few days after the declaration of war.

'How old is the princess today?'

'Let me just work it out . . . She is five or six years

younger than my uncle ... So, seventy-one or seventy-two ...'

'Did she come here often?'

'I've never seen her here. I don't think she ever set foot here, or if she did it was before.'

'Before what?'

'Before she married the Prince of V—.'

'Listen, Monsieur Mazeron. I would like you to tell me this story as clearly as possible ...'

'Isabelle was the daughter of the Duke of S—.'

It was strange, hearing in real life names he had learned in French history.

'And so?'

'My uncle was twenty-six, in about 1910, when he met her. More precisely, he had known her as a little girl, in the duke's chateau, where he sometimes spent the summer holidays. Then for a long time he didn't see her, and when they met up once again they fell in love with each other.'

'Had your uncle already lost his father?'

'Two years previously.'

'Did he inherit a large fortune?'

'Only this house and some land in the Sologne.'

'Why didn't they get married?'

'I don't know. Perhaps because my uncle was starting out in the diplomatic corps, and he was sent to Poland as a second or third secretary at the embassy.'

'Were they engaged?'

'No.'

Maigret felt it was slightly indecent leafing through the letters scattered in front of him. Contrary to his expectations, they were not love letters. In quite a lively style, the girl who had written them related the minor events of her own life and the life of Paris.

She did not address her correspondent by the familiar *tu*, calling him her 'great friend', and signed her letters: 'your faithful Isi'.

'Then what happened?'

'Before the war – I mean the First War – in 1912, if I'm not mistaken, Isabelle married the Prince of V—.'

'Did she love him?'

'If we believe what they say, no. They even claim that she frankly admitted as much to him. All I know about it is what I heard my father and mother saying about it when I was a child.'

'Your mother was the sister of the Count of Saint-Hilaire?'

'Yes.'

'She didn't marry into her milieu?'

'She married my father, who was a painter and who enjoyed a certain success at the time. He is rather forgotten now, but you will still find one of his paintings at the Palais de Luxembourg. Later, to make a living, he became a picture restorer.'

During that part of the morning, Maigret had had a sense of pulling out each bit of the truth almost by force. He couldn't get a clear image of it. These people struck him as unreal, as if they had sprung from the pages of a turn-of-the-century novel.

'If I understand correctly, Armand de Saint-Hilaire didn't marry Isabelle because his fortune was too small?'

'I suppose so, yes. That's what I was frequently told, and what seems most likely to me.'

'So she married the Prince of V—, whom she didn't love, as you say, and to whom she had honestly confessed as much.'

'It was an arrangement between two great families, between two great names.'

Hadn't the Saint-Fiacres done similar things in the old days, and, when they wanted to find a wife for her son, hadn't the old countess turned to her bishop?

'Did the couple have children?'

'Just one, after several years of marriage.'

'What happened to him?'

'Prince Philippe must be forty-five now. He married a girl called de Marchangy and lives almost the whole year in his chateau at Genestoux, near Caen, where he has a stud and some farms. He has five or six children.'

'For about fifty years, judging by this correspondence, Isabelle and your uncle went on writing to each other. Almost every day they wrote each other letters several pages long. Was the husband aware of this?'

'They say so.'

'Do you know him?'

'Only by sight.'

'What sort of man is he?'

'A gentleman and a collector.'

'A collector of what?'

'Of medals, of snuffboxes . . .'

'He moved in society circles?'

'He had people to dinner every week, in his townhouse

on Rue de Varenne and, in the autumn, at his chateau at Saint-Sauveur-en-Bourbonnais.'

Maigret had raised an eyebrow. On the one hand he felt that it was probably true, but at the same time the characters struck him as unreal.

'Rue de Varenne,' he objected, 'is five minutes' walk from here.'

'And yet I would be willing to swear that for fifty years my uncle and the princess never met.'

'Even though they wrote to each other every day?'

'You have the letters right in front of you.'

'And the husband knew about it?'

'Isabelle would never have agreed to writing in secret.'

Maigret had almost felt like losing his temper, as if he were being made fun of. And yet the letters were right in front of him, in fact, and full of revealing phrases.

. . . this morning, at eleven o'clock, I received a visit from Abbé Gauge, and we talked a lot about you. It's a comfort to me to know that the bonds connecting us are those that men cannot sunder . . .

'Is the princess very Catholic?'

'She had a chapel blessed in the house on Rue de Varenne.'

'And her husband?'

'He's Catholic too.'

'Did he have mistresses?'

'That's what they claim.'

Another letter, from a more recent bundle:

. . . I will be grateful all my life to Hubert for understanding . . .

'I assume Hubert is the Prince of V——?'
'Yes. He used to belong to the Cadre Noir de Saumur, the corps of riding instructors. He still rode in the Bois de Boulogne every morning, until he had a bad fall last week.'
'What age was he?'
'Eighty.'
This affair involved only old people, who had relationships that did not seem human.
'Are you sure of everything you are telling me, Monsieur Mazeron?'
'If you doubt me, ask anyone.'
Anyone in a milieu of which Maigret had only a vague and certainly imprecise idea!
'Let's keep going!' he had sighed wearily. 'That prince is the one who has recently died, as you told me just now?'
'On Sunday morning, yes. It was in the papers. He died of his injuries after falling from his horse, and the funeral will be happening right now at Sainte-Clotilde.'
'He had no relationship with your uncle?'
'Not that I know of.'
'And what if they met in society?'
'I suppose they avoided frequenting the same salons and the same circles.'
'Did they hate each other?'
'I don't think so.'
'Did your uncle ever talk to you about the prince?'
'No. He never mentioned him.'

'And about Isabelle?'

'He told me a long time ago that I was his sole heir, and that it was a shame that I didn't bear his name. He was also saddened by the fact that I had no sons, only two daughters. If I had had a son, he added, he would have requested a ruling allowing him to bear the name of Saint-Hilaire.'

'So you are your uncle's sole heir.'

'Yes. I haven't finished my story. Indirectly, without mentioning any names, he talked to me that time about the princess. What he said was:

'"I still hope to marry one day, God alone knows when, and it will be too late for us to have children . . ."'

'If I understand correctly, the situation is this. In about 1912, your uncle met a girl whom he loved and who loved him, but they didn't get married because the Count of Saint-Hilaire barely had a fortune.'

'That's exactly right.'

'Two years later, while your uncle is in Poland or in an embassy somewhere else, young Isabelle has a marriage of convenience and becomes the Princess of V—. She has a son, so it isn't a mere formality. The couple behaved, at the time at least, as husband and wife.'

'Yes.'

'Unless Isabelle and your uncle met up in the meantime and yielded to their passion.'

'No.'

'Why are you so categorical? Do you think that in that world . . .'

'I say no because my uncle spent the whole of the First

War outside of France and when he came back, the child, Philippe, was two or three years old.'

'Let's admit it. Lovers see each other . . .'

'No.'

'They never saw each other?'

'I already told you.'

'So for fifty years they write to each other almost daily, and, one day, your uncle tells you about a marriage that will take place in a more or less distant future. Which means, I imagine, that he and Isabelle were waiting for the prince to die so that they could get married.'

'I think so.'

Maigret had wiped his brow and looked at the lime tree outside the French windows, as if he needed to resume contact with a more grounded reality.

'We're reaching the epilogue. Ten or twelve days ago, it doesn't matter which, the eighty-year-old prince falls from his horse in the Bois de Boulogne. On Sunday morning he dies of his injuries. Yesterday, Tuesday, or two days later, your uncle is murdered, in the evening, in his office. The consequence of this is that the couple who have waited for fifty years to be united at last will not be. Is that right? Thank you, Monsieur Mazeron. Would you please be so kind as to give me your wife's address?'

'23, Rue de la Pompe, in Passy.'

'Do you know your uncle's notary or lawyer?'

'His notary is Maître Aubonnet, on Rue de Villersexel.'

A few hundred metres away. Those people, apart from Madame Mazeron, lived almost next door to each other, in the part of Paris that Maigret knew least.

'You are free to go. I assume I can always contact you at your home?'

'I won't be there very much this afternoon, because I have to take care of the funeral, the announcements, and above all I need to contact Maître Aubonnet.'

Mazeron had left unwillingly, and Jaquette had burst out of the kitchen and closed the door behind him.

'Do you need me now?'

'Not right away. It's lunchtime. We'll come back this afternoon.'

'Do I have to stay here?'

'Where would you go?'

She had looked at him uncomprehendingly.

'I'm asking you where you wanted to go.'

'Me? Nowhere. Where would I go?'

Because of her attitude, Maigret and Janvier had not left straight away. Maigret had called Quai des Orfèvres.

'Lucas? Have you got someone to hand who could come and spend an hour or two at Rue Saint-Dominique? Torrence? Fine. Get him to jump in a car . . .'

Consequently, while the two men had lunch, Torrence was snoozing in the Count of Saint-Hilaire's armchair.

As far as anyone could tell, nothing had been stolen from the flat. There had been no break-in. The murderer had come in through the door and, since Jaquette swore that she hadn't let anyone in, they had to believe that the count himself had opened the door to his visitor.

Did he expect him? Did he not expect him? He hadn't offered him a drink. They had found only a single glass, on the desk, beside the bottle of cognac.

Would Saint-Hilaire have stayed in his dressing gown to receive a woman? Probably not, if they were able to rely a little on what they knew of him.

So it was a man who had come to see him. The count was not suspicious of him, because he had sat down at his desk, by the proofs that he had been busy correcting a moment before.

'Did you notice whether there were any cigarette butts in the ashtray?'

'I don't think so.'

'Or cigar butts?'

'None of those either.'

'I bet that before this evening we will have a phone call from young Monsieur Cromières.'

Another one with the gift of infuriating Maigret.

'The prince's funeral must be over.'

'That's quite likely.'

'So Isabelle is at her house, Rue de Varenne, surrounded by her son, her daughter-in-law and their children.'

Silence fell. Maigret frowned, as if hesitating.

'Do you plan to go and see them?' Janvier asked with a hint of concern.

'No . . . Not with those people . . . Will you have a coffee? Waiter! Two black coffees.'

It looked as if he was furious with everyone today, including the more or less high-ranking civil servants who were eating at the nearby tables and observing him ironically.

3.

As soon as he had turned the corner of Rue Saint-Dominique, Maigret saw them and groaned. There were a good dozen of them, journalists and photographers, standing outside the home of the Count of Saint-Hilaire, and some of them, as if preparing for a lengthy siege, were sitting on the pavement with their backs to the wall.

They had recognized him in the distance as well and hurried towards him.

'Our dear Monsieur Cromières is going to love this!' he muttered to Janvier.

It was inevitable. Whenever a case was dealt with by a local station, someone always alerted the press.

The photographers, who had a hundred pictures of him in their files, snapped away at him as if he had changed since the previous day, or any other day. The reporters asked questions. Luckily they revealed that they knew less than one might have feared.

'Is it a suicide, inspector?'

'Have any papers disappeared?'

'For now, gentlemen, I have nothing to say.'

'Should we conclude that it might be a political matter?'

They walked backwards in front of him, clutching their notebooks.

'When will you be able to give us a clue?'

'Maybe tomorrow, maybe in a week.'

He had the misfortune of adding:

'Maybe never.'

He tried to retract his mistake:

'I'm joking, of course. Please be so kind as to let us work in peace.'

'Is it true that he was writing his memoirs?'

'Indeed, two volumes have already been published.'

A uniformed officer was standing outside the door. A few moments later, after Maigret rang at the door, Torrence, in his shirt-sleeves, came and opened it.

'I was obliged to call a local sergeant, chief. They had got into the building and thought it was amusing to keep ringing the bell every five minutes.'

'Any news? Phone calls?'

'About twenty. Newspapers.'

'Where's the old woman?'

'In the kitchen. Every time the phone rings she hurries in the hope of answering before I do. The first time, she tried to grab the receiver out of my hands.'

'She herself hasn't made any calls? You know there's a second phone in the bedroom?'

'I've left the door of the office open to hear her movements. She hasn't gone into the bedroom.'

'She hasn't gone out?'

'No. She tried to go out to get some fresh bread, she told me. As you didn't give me any instructions on the subject, I decided to prevent her. What should I do now?'

'Go back to Quai des Orfèvres.'

For a moment the inspector had considered going back there too, and taking Jaquette to question her at leisure. But he didn't feel ready for this interrogation. He decided instead to linger in the flat, and in the end he would probably try to get the old maidservant to speak in Saint-Hilaire's office.

While waiting, he opened the tall double French windows and sat down in the chair that the count had occupied so often. His hand was reaching out towards a bundle of letters when the door opened. It was Jaquette Larrieu, more sour and more suspicious than ever.

'You have no right to do that.'

'You know who these letters are from?'

'It doesn't much matter whether I know or I don't. It's private correspondence.'

'Please do me the favour of going back into the kitchen or your bedroom.'

'I'm not allowed to go out?'

'Not for now.'

She hesitated, trying to come up with a cutting reply, which she didn't find, and, pale with rage, she resigned herself to leaving the office.

'Go and find me the silver-framed photograph that I noticed in the bedroom this morning.'

That morning, Maigret hadn't paid very much attention. Too many things were still alien to him. It was a matter of principle to him not to try to form an opinion too quickly, because he mistrusted first impressions.

Over lunch outside the restaurant, he had suddenly remembered a lithograph that he had seen for years in his parents' bedroom. It must have been his mother who had chosen it and hung it up. The frame was white, in the style of the early years of the century. It showed a young woman by a lake, wearing a princess dress, a wide-brimmed hat with an ostrich-feather on her head and a pointed parasol in her hand. The expression on her face was melancholy, like the landscape, and Maigret was sure that his mother found the picture poetic. Wasn't it the poetry of the times?

The story of Isabelle and the Count of Saint-Hilaire had recalled that picture so precisely to his memory that he could even see the wallpaper with the pale-blue stripes in his parents' bedroom.

And yet, in the silver frame that he had noticed that morning in the count's bedroom, and which Janvier was bringing him now, he saw the same outline, the same style of dress and an identical melancholy.

He had no doubt that it was a photograph of Isabelle in about 1912, the time when she was still a girl, and when the future ambassador had first met her.

She wasn't tall and, perhaps because of her corset, she seemed to have a slender waist, and her bosom was, as they said in those days, ample. Her features were delicately drawn, her mouth thin, her eyes clear, blue or grey.

'What do you want me to do, chief?'

'Sit down.'

He needed someone there, as if to check his impressions. In front of him, the bundles of letters were arranged by the year, and he picked them up one after another. He didn't read everything, of course, because it would have taken several days, just odd passages here and there.

'My handsome friend ... Very dear friend ... Sweet friend ...'

Later, perhaps because she felt herself to be in a closer communion with her correspondent, she wrote simply: 'Friend'.

Saint-Hilaire had kept the envelopes, which bore stamps from different countries. Isabelle had moved around a lot. For a long time, for example, the letters from the month of August were sent from Baden-Baden or Marienbad, the aristocratic spa towns of the day.

There were also some sent from the Tyrol, many from Switzerland and Portugal. She related the small events that filled her days with charm and vivacity and described quite wittily the people she met.

Often she referred to them only by their first names, sometimes by a simple initial.

It took Maigret some time to find his bearings. Helped by the postage stamp and the context, he gradually managed to decipher these puzzles.

Marie, for example, was a queen who was still on the throne at the time, the queen of Romania. It was from Bucharest, where she was staying at the court with her father, that Isabelle wrote, and a year later she was to be found again at the Italian court.

'My cousin H ...'

The name returned in its entirety in another letter, the Prince of Hessen, and there were others, more or less cousins or second cousins.

During the First War, she sent her letters via the French embassy in Madrid.

My father explained to me yesterday that I must marry the Prince of V—, whom you have met at my house several times. I asked him for three days to reflect and, during those three days, I cried a lot . . .

Maigret puffed on his pipe, sometimes glancing at the garden, at the leaves of the lime tree, and passed the letters one by one to Janvier, keeping an eye on his reactions.

He was faintly irritated by these descriptions, which struck him as so unreal. Had he not looked, as a child, with similar unease, at the woman by the lake in his parents' bedroom? In his eyes it was a false poetry: she was an unreal and impossible creature.

And yet here, in a world that had evolved still further, had become harsher, he found an almost identical image.

This afternoon I had a long conversation with Hubert, and I was completely frank. He knows I love you, that too many obstacles keep us apart, and that I bow to my father's will . . .

Only the previous week, Maigret had dealt with a simple and brutal crime of passion, a lover who had stabbed to death the husband of the woman he loved, and who had then killed the woman before at last trying unsuccessfully to slash his own wrists. Admittedly these were just ordinary people of the Faubourg Saint-Antoine.

46

He has accepted that our marriage will be one of convenience, and I promised for my part never to see you again.
He doesn't know that I am writing to you. He holds you
in high esteem and does not doubt the respect that you
have always shown towards me . . .

There were moments when Maigret was revolted, felt an
almost physical revulsion.

'Do you believe it, Janvier?'

'It sounds as if she's being sincere . . .'

'Read this one!'

It was three years later.

I know, dear friend, that you will suffer, but, if it is any
consolation I am suffering even more than you.

This was in 1915. She was announcing that Julien, the
brother of the Prince of V—, had been killed in Argonne
at the head of his regiment. She had, once more, had a
long conversation with her husband, who had come back
to Paris on leave. What she was telling the man she loved,
quite clearly, was that she was going to be obliged to
sleep with the prince. Of course, she didn't use those
terms. Not only was there no crude or shocking word in
her letter, but the very fact was presented in an almost
unreal manner.

While Julien was still alive, Hubert was not worried,
being convinced that his brother would have an heir, and
that the name of V— would thus . . .

There was no longer a brother. So it was Hubert's duty to ensure that there was a descendant.

> I spent the night in prayer, and in the morning I went to see my spiritual adviser . . .

The priest had shared the view of the prince. One could not, for a question of love, allow a name that had been found on every page of the history of France to fade away.

> I have understood my duty . . .

The sacrifice had been made because a child, Philippe, had been born. She also announced this birth, and on this subject there were a few words that made Maigret think:

> Thank God! It's a boy . . .

Didn't that mean, in black and white, that if the child had been a girl she would have had to start over again?

And if she had had another daughter, and then another . . .

'Have you read it?'

'Yes.'

It was almost as if they were both prey to the same unease. They were both used to quite a crude reality, and the passions they came across ended in tragedy because they led to Quai des Orfèvres.

This, on the other hand, was as disappointing as trying to grasp a cloud. And when they tried to make out the characters, they remained as vague, as inconsistent as the lady of the lake.

Maigret was tempted just to stuff all those letters into the bookcase with the green curtain, muttering:

'Heap of nonsense!'

At the same time he felt a certain respect and almost tenderness. Not wanting to yield to sentimentality, he tried to act tough.

'Can you believe it?'

More dukes, princes and dethroned kings that she had met in Portugal. Then a trip to Kenya, with her husband. Another trip, to the United States, where Isabelle had felt lost, because the life there was too brutal.

> . . . The more he grows, the more like you Philippe becomes. Isn't that miraculous? Isn't it as if heaven were trying to reward us for our sacrifice? Hubert is aware of it as well, I can see it in the way that he looks at the child . . .

Hubert, at any rate, was no longer allowed in the marital bed, and he had no hesitation in seeking consolation elsewhere. In his letters, he was now no longer Hubert, but H . . .

> Poor H. has a new folly and I suspect that it is making him suffer. He is growing visibly thinner, and more and more nervous . . .

'Follies' of this kind appeared every five or six months. For his part, Armand de Saint-Hilaire, in his own letters, could not have been trying to convince his correspondent of his own continence.

Isabelle wrote to him, for example:

I hope that the Turkish women are less wild than people say, and particularly that their husbands are not too fierce . . .

She added:

Be careful, friend. I pray for you every morning . . .

When he was an envoy in Cuba, and then ambassador in Buenos Aires, she worried about the Spanish-blooded women.

They are so beautiful! And I, far away and far from view, tremble at the idea that you might one day fall in love . . .

She was worried about his health.

Are your boils still giving you trouble? With that heat, it must . . .

She knew Jaquette.

I am writing to Jaquette to give her the recipe of the almond tart that you like so much . . .

'Hadn't she promised her husband that she wouldn't see

Saint-Hilaire again . . . ? Listen to this . . . It was sent to this address:

' "What happiness, at once painful and ineffable, to see you in the distance at the Opéra . . . I love your greying temples, and that slight paunch lends you an unparalleled dignity . . . I was proud of you all evening . . .

' "It was only when I got back to Rue de Varenne and looked in my mirror that I was frightened. How could I have failed to disappoint you . . . ? Women fade quickly, and I am nearly an old woman . . ." '

They had seen each other like that, in the distance, on quite a large number of occasions. They even arranged meetings of a kind.

Tomorrow, at about three o'clock, I will be walking in the Tuileries with my son . . .

Saint-Hilaire, for his part, passed below her windows at times of day that were agreed in advance.

On the subject of her son, while he was about ten years old, there was a characteristic phrase that Maigret read out loud.

' "Philippe, finding me writing once again, asked me candidly: 'Are you writing to your lover again?' " '

Maigret sighed and mopped his brow, then tied up the bundles again, one after the other.

'Try to get Dr Tudelle on the phone for me.'

He needed to find himself back on solid ground. The letters were returned to their place in the bookcase, and he promised himself that he wouldn't touch them again.

'He's on the line, chief . . .'

'Hello, doctor . . . Maigret, yes . . . You finished ten minutes ago . . . ? No, of course, I won't ask you for all the details . . .'

While listening, he scribbled down some words, meaningless marks, on Saint-Hilaire's pad.

'Are you sure? You have already sent the bullets to Gastinne-Renette? I'll call him a little later . . . Thank you . . . It would be better if you sent the report to the examining magistrate . . . He'll be glad of that . . . Thanks again.'

He started pacing around the room, his hands behind his back, stopping from time to time to look at the garden, where an unconcerned blackbird was hopping in the grass a few feet away from him.

'The first bullet,' he explained to Janvier, 'was fired head on, almost point-blank . . . It's a 7.65 bullet with a nickel-plated jacket . . . Tudelle isn't yet as experienced as Dr Paul, but he is more or less sure that it was fired from a Browning automatic . . . He is categorical on one point: that first bullet was the almost instantaneous cause of death. The body leaned forward and slipped from the armchair to the rug . . .'

'How does he know?'

'Because the other shots were fired downwards.'

'How many others?'

'Three. Two to the belly and one to the shoulder. Automatic pistols contain six cartridges, or seven if one had slipped into the barrel, so I wonder why the murderer stopped suddenly after the fourth bullet. Unless the pistol jammed . . .'

He looked at the rug, which had been given a bit of a clean, but on which one could still make out the outline of bloodstains.

'Either the perpetrator wanted to be sure that his victim was dead or he was in such a state of excitement that he went on mechanically firing. Call Moers for me, will you?'

That morning he had been too gripped by the strange aspect of the case to pay attention to physical clues and had left that task to the specialists from Criminal Records.

'Moers? Yes . . . How far have you got? Of course . . . First of all, tell me if you found any cartridge cases in the office . . . No? . . . None?'

It was odd, and it seemed to indicate that the murderer knew he wouldn't be disturbed. After four noisy explosions, very noisy if the gun was a Browning 7.65, he had taken the time to look around the room for cartridge cases that had been ejected quite some distance.

'The door handle?'

'The only more or less clean prints belonged to the housekeeper.'

'The glass?'

'The dead man's prints.'

'The desk, the furniture?'

'Nothing, chief. I mean no unfamiliar prints apart from yours.'

'The lock, the windows?'

'Photographic enlargements show no sign of a break-in.'

Perhaps Isabelle's letters weren't like the love letters that Maigret normally dealt with, but the crime was real enough.

Yet two details appeared at first sight to contradict one

another. The murderer had gone on firing at a corpse, a man who had stopped moving and who, with his shattered skull, presented quite a horrid spectacle. Maigret remembered the still abundant white hair sticking to the gaping cranium, one eye still open, a bone protruding from the torn cheek.

The pathologist affirmed that after the first shot the corpse was on the ground, at the foot of the armchair, in the spot where it had been found.

So the murderer, who was probably on the other side of the desk, had come around it to shoot again, once, twice, three times, downwards, at close range, less than fifty centimetres, according to Tudelle.

At that distance there was no need to aim to hit a precise point. In other words, the chest and the belly had been shot deliberately.

Did that not suggest revenge or an unusual level of hatred?

'Are you sure there's no gun in the apartment? Have you searched everywhere?'

'Not even in the chimney,' Janvier replied.

Maigret too had looked for the automatic that the housekeeper had talked about, albeit in quite vague terms.

'Go and ask the officer stationed outside the door if he happens to have a 7.65 in his belt.'

Many uniformed officers were equipped with a weapon of that calibre.

'Ask him to lend it to you for a moment.'

He left the office too, walked across the corridor and pushed open the door of the kitchen, where Jaquette

Larrieu was sitting straight-backed on a chair. Her eyes closed, she looked as if she was sleeping. She gave a start at the sound.

'Will you follow me . . .'

'Where to?'

'The office. I have a few questions I would like to ask you.'

'I've already told you that I don't know anything.'

Once she was in the room, she looked around as if to check that nothing had been disturbed.

'Take a seat.'

She hesitated, probably unused to sitting down in this room in the presence of her employer.

'On this chair . . . There you are.'

She reluctantly obeyed and gave the inspector a more suspicious look than ever.

Janvier came back, holding an automatic.

'Give it to her.'

She couldn't bear to take it, opened her mouth to speak, closed it again, and Maigret could have sworn that she nearly said:

'Where did you find it?'

She was fascinated by the gun. She had difficulty taking her eyes off it.

'Do you recognize this pistol?'

'How could I recognize it? I've never examined it from close to, and I can't imagine they only made one like it.'

'Is this the kind of gun that the count owned?'

'I suppose so.'

'The same size?'

'I have no idea.'

'Take it in your hand. Is it about the same weight?'

She refused outright to do what was asked of her.

'There would be no point, because I've never touched the one that was in the drawer.'

'You can take it back to the officer, Janvier.'

'You don't need me any more?'

'Please stay. I assume you don't know if your employer gave or lent his pistol to anyone, his nephew, for example, or anyone else?'

'How would I know? All I know is that I haven't seen it for a long time.'

'Was the Count of Saint-Hilaire afraid of robbers?'

'Certainly not. Not robbers, not murderers. The proof is that in the summer he slept with the window open, even though we are on the ground floor and anybody could have got into the bedroom.'

'And he didn't keep any valuable objects in the apartment?'

'You and your men know better than I do what there is here.'

'When did you go into service with him?'

'Immediately after the First War. He was coming back from abroad. His manservant had died.'

'So you were in your twenties?'

'Twenty-eight.'

'How long had you been in Paris?'

'A few months. Before that I lived with my father in Normandy. When my father died, I was obliged to work.'

'Did you have love affairs?'

'I'm sorry?'

'I'm asking if you had lovers or a fiancé.'

She looked at him resentfully.

'You're barking up the wrong tree.'

'So you lived alone with the Count of Saint-Hilaire in his apartment?'

'Is there anything wrong with that?'

Maigret wasn't necessarily following a logical order, because nothing struck him as logical in this case, and he moved from one subject to another as if looking for the sore spot. Janvier, having come back into the room, had sat down near the door. As he lit a cigarette and dropped the match on the floor, the old woman, who didn't miss a thing, told him off.

'You could use an ashtray.'

'By the way, did your employer smoke?'

'He smoked for a long time.'

'Cigarettes?'

'Cigars.'

'And recently, had he stopped smoking?'

'Yes. Because of his chronic bronchitis.'

'But he seemed to be in excellent health.'

Dr Tudelle had told Maigret on the telephone that Saint-Hilaire must have enjoyed exceptionally good health.

'A solid frame, a heart in perfect condition, no sclerosis.'

But some of his organs were too severely damaged by bullets to allow a complete diagnosis.

'When you went into his service, he was almost a young man.'

'He was three years older than me.'

'Did you know that he was in love?'

'I took his letters to the post office.'

'You weren't jealous?'

'Why would I have been jealous?'

'Didn't you ever see the person he wrote to every day?'

'She never set foot in the flat.'

'But you saw her?'

She fell silent.

'Tell me. When the case goes to the Court of Assizes, you will be asked more embarrassing questions than that, and you won't be allowed to say nothing.'

'I don't know anything.'

'I asked you if you had seen this person.'

'Yes. She passed along the street. I sometimes delivered letters that he sent to her in person.'

'Secretly?'

'No. I asked to see her and I was shown into her apartment.'

'Did she speak to you?'

'Sometimes she asked me questions.'

'You're talking about forty years ago?'

'Then and more recently.'

'What kind of questions?'

'Mostly about the count's health.'

'Not about the people he had over for dinner?'

'No.'

'Did you follow your employer abroad?'

'Everywhere!'

'As a minister, then as an ambassador, he was obliged to keep a large household. What was your precise role?'

'I looked after him.'

'You mean that you weren't on the same footing as the other servants, that you didn't have to deal with cooking, cleaning, receptions?'

'I kept an eye.'

'What was your title? Housekeeper?'

'I had no title.'

'Did you have lovers?'

She stiffened, her face more contemptuous than ever.

'Were you his mistress?'

Maigret worried that she was about to pounce on him with all her claws out.

'I know from his correspondence,' he went on, 'that he had love affairs.'

'He had every right, didn't he?'

'Were you jealous?'

'Sometimes I threw certain people out of the door, because they weren't right for him and would have caused him problems.'

'In other words, you took care of his private life.'

'He was too good, too naive.'

'But he carried out the delicate role of ambassador with great distinction.'

'It's not the same thing.'

'Did you ever leave him?'

'Is that mentioned in the letters?'

It was Maigret's turn not to reply, but to continue:

'For how long were you parted from him?'

'Five months.'

'When was that?'

'When he was an envoy in Cuba.'

'Why?'

'Because of a woman who demanded that he put me out of the house.'

'What kind of woman?'

Silence.

'Why couldn't she bear you? Did she live with him?'

'She came to see him every day and often spent the night at the residence.'

'Where did you go?'

'I rented a little lodging near the Paseo del Prado.'

'Did your employer visit you there?'

'He didn't dare to, he merely phoned me to mollify me. He knew it wouldn't last. I still bought my ticket back to Europe.'

'But you didn't leave?'

'He came to see me the day before I was due to leave.'

'Did you know Prince Philippe?'

'If you have really read the letters, you don't need to ask me. It shouldn't be allowed, looking through people's correspondence after they die.'

'You didn't answer the question.'

'I saw him when he was young.'

'Where?'

'Rue de Varenne. He often went to see his mother.'

'It didn't occur to you to phone the princess this morning, before going to Quai d'Orsay?'

She looked at him without batting an eyelid.

'Why didn't you do that when, by your own account, you acted for a long time as an intermediary between the two?'

'Because it's the day of the funeral.'

'And afterwards, this morning, while we were out, you weren't tempted to inform her?'

She stared at the telephone.

'There was always someone in the office.'

There was a knock at the door. It was the policeman on duty on the pavement.

'I don't know if this is of interest. I thought I should bring you the paper.'

It was an afternoon daily, which must have come out an hour before. A headline in quite big letters, at the bottom of the front page, announced:

MYSTERIOUS DEATH OF AN AMBASSADOR

It was a short article.

This morning the body of Count Armand de Saint-Hilaire, for a long time the French ambassador in various capital cities, including Rome, London and Washington, was found at his home in Rue Saint-Dominique.

Having retired several years ago, Armand de Saint-Hilaire has published two volumes of memoirs and was correcting the proofs of a third volume when he appears to have been murdered.

The crime was discovered early this morning by an elderly housekeeper.

It is not yet known whether the motive was robbery, or whether more mysterious reasons are yet to be found.

He held out the newspaper to Jaquette and looked hesitantly at the telephone. He was wondering whether they had read the newspaper at Rue de Varenne, or whether anyone had told Isabelle the news.

In that case, how would she react? Would she dare come in person? Would she send her son for information? Would she merely wait, in the silence of her townhouse, where they had probably closed the shutters as a sign of mourning?

Shouldn't Maigret . . .

He got to his feet, annoyed with everything, and went and stood looking at the garden, tapping his pipe against his heel to empty it, much to Jaquette's indignation.

4.

The old maid, tiny and stiff on her chair, listened with horror to the inspector's voice, which was filled with inflections that she had not heard before. However, Maigret was addressing not her but an unseen person at the other end of the line.

'No, Monsieur Cromières, I haven't sent out a press release, and I haven't invited either journalists or photographers, as gentlemen from the ministries do at the drop of a hat. As to your second question, I have nothing else to tell you, nor any idea, as you say, but if I discover something I will immediately give a report to the examining magistrate . . .'

He caught Jaquette glancing covertly at Janvier. She seemed to be taking him as witness to Maigret's ill-contained rage, and there was a faint smile on her lips, a little as if she had said to the inspector:

'Well, your boss . . .'

Maigret dragged his companion into the corridor.

'I'm going to call in on the notary. Keep asking her questions, without pressing her too much, nicely, you know what I mean. Perhaps you'll have more luck charming her than I have had.'

It was true. If he had predicted that morning that he would be dealing with a stubborn old maid, he would have brought along young Lapointe rather than Janvier, because out of everyone in the Police Judiciaire it was Lapointe who enjoyed the greatest success with women of a certain age. Hadn't one of them said, shaking her head: 'I wonder how such a well-brought-up young man can do this job . . .'

She had added:

'I'm sure it causes you pain.'

Maigret found himself back in the street, where the journalists had only left one of their own on sentry duty while they went to refresh themselves in a local bistro.

'No news, my friend. No point in following me.'

He didn't go far. You never had to go far in this case. It seemed as if, for everyone involved, closely or otherwise, Paris was no more than a small number of aristocratic streets.

The notary's house in Rue de Villersexel was of the same period and style as the one in Rue Saint-Dominique; it too had a coach-gate, a huge red-carpeted staircase and a lift that probably rose smoothly and silently. He didn't need to take it, because the practice was on the first floor. The brass buttons on the double door were well polished, as was the plaque inviting visitors to come in without ringing.

'If I find myself face to face with another old man . . .'

He was pleasantly surprised to see, among the clerks, a pretty woman in her thirties.

'Maître Aubonnet, please.'

Admittedly the office was rather muffled, and just a tad solemn, but he wasn't kept waiting and was ushered almost immediately into an enormous room where a man barely forty-five years of age got up to welcome him.

'Detective Chief Inspector Maigret . . . I've come to see you about one of your clients, the Count of Saint-Hilaire . . .'

And the man replied with a smile:

'In that case it's not me you want to speak to but my father. I'll just see if he's free right now.'

Monsieur Aubonnet the younger went into another room and stayed there for a while.

'If you'd like to come through, Monsieur Maigret . . .'

This time, of course, the inspector found himself in the presence of a real old man, who wasn't even in particularly good shape. Aubonnet Senior sat, eyelids twitching, in the depths of a high-backed armchair, wearing the irritable expression of a man who has just been dragged from his afternoon nap.

'Speak quite loudly,' the son advised as he withdrew.

Maître Aubonnet must once have been very fat. He had kept a certain paunch, but his body was soft, with wrinkles everywhere. One foot wore a shoe, the other, with a swollen ankle, a felt slipper.

'I suppose you've come to talk to me about my poor friend?'

His mouth was soft too, and the syllables that issued from it formed a kind of mush. On the other hand, Maigret didn't need to ask him questions to unleash his chatter.

'Just imagine, Saint-Hilaire and I met at Stanislas . . . How long ago is that? . . . Wait . . . I'm seventy-seven. So that's sixty years since we were in Upper Sixth together.

He was destined for the diplomatic corps. My dream was to join the Cadre Noir de Saumur . . . There were still horses in those days. The cavalry weren't motorized . . . Do you know that I've never in my life had the opportunity to ride horses? All because I was an only son and had to take over my father's practice . . .'

Maigret didn't ask him if his father lived in the same house.

'Saint-Hilaire, from school onwards, was someone who enjoyed life, but he was quite a rare kind of bon viveur, elegant to his fingertips . . .'

'I assume he left his will in your hands.'

'His nephew, young Mazeron, asked me the same question just now. I reassured him . . .'

'Does the nephew inherit all his possessions?'

'Not all of them, no. I know the will by heart, because it was drafted with my own hand.'

'A long time ago?'

'The last one dates from about ten years ago.'

'Were the previous wills different?'

'Only in terms of details. I wasn't able to show the document to the nephew, given that all interested parties have to be present.'

'Who are they?'

'Broadly speaking, Alain Mazeron inherits the building on Rue Saint-Dominique and, in general, the fortune, which isn't very large. Jaquette Larrieu, the housekeeper, receives a lifelong pension, which will allow her to end her days in comfort. As to the furniture, knick-knacks, paintings, personal objects, Saint-Hilaire leaves them to an old friend . . .'

'Isabelle de V——.'

'I can see that you are well informed.'

'Do you know her?'

'Quite well. I was better acquainted with her husband, who was a client of mine.'

Wasn't it quite surprising to see the two men choosing the same notary?

'Weren't they afraid of bumping into each other in your practice?'

'It never happened. Probably they never thought about it, and I wonder if it would really have been awkward for them. You see, they were made, if not to be friends, then at least to esteem one another, because they were both men of honour, and also men of taste.'

These seemed to be words from a bygone era! It was a long time, in fact, since Maigret had heard the expression *man of honour*.

The old notary, in his armchair, laughed silently at a fleeting thought.

'Men of taste, yes!' he repeated mischievously. 'One might add that in one aspect of life their tastes were identical . . . Now that they are dead, I don't think I'll be breaking client confidentiality if I tell you this, particularly since you too are obliged to remain silent on the matter. A notary is almost always a confidant . . . Saint-Hilaire was also an old friend who came to tell me of his escapades . . . For almost a year, he and the prince had the same mistress, a pretty girl with an opulent bosom, who acted in I can't remember which revue on the Boulevards . . . They didn't know . . . Each one had his day . . .'

The old man gave Maigret a bawdy look.

'Those people know how to live . . . For several years I have barely attended to my practice, where my elder son has taken my place. But I come down to my office every day, and continue to serve my former clients.'

'Did Saint-Hilaire have friends?'

'The situation with his friends is the same as with the clients I'm talking to you about. At our age, you see people dying one after another. I think that by the end I was the last one he visited. He had kept a good pair of legs and still took his walk every day. Sometimes he came up to see me, to sit where you are sitting . . .'

'What did you talk about?'

'About the old days, of course, particularly the time spent at Stanislas. I could still tell you most of the names of our fellow pupils. It's astonishing, the number who had outstanding careers. One of our classmates, not the most intelligent, was president of the Council I don't know how many times and only died last year. Another is a member of the Academy, in a military capacity . . .'

'Had Saint-Hilaire made any enemies?'

'How would he have done that? In his professional life he never ran up against anyone, as is so often the case these days. He obtained his positions by waiting patiently for his turn. And in his memoirs he never settled any scores, which explains why so few people read them . . .'

'And among the Prince of V—'s family?'

The notary looked at him with surprise.

'I've already talked to you about the prince. He knew what was going on, of course, and he knew that

Saint-Hilaire would keep his word. If it hadn't been for the world, I'm sure that Armand would have had him over to Rue de Varenne, and that he might well have invited him to dinner.'

'Was the son aware as well?'

'Certainly.'

'What sort of man is he?'

'I don't think he's of the same calibre as his father. It's true, I don't know him as well. He seems more reserved, which might be explained by the difficulty in our time of bearing such a weighty name as his. He isn't interested in high society. He isn't seen often in Paris. He spends most of the year in Normandy, with his wife and children, looking after his farms and his horses . . .'

'Have you seen him recently?'

'I will see him tomorrow, as well as his mother, for the reading of the will, which means that I will probably have to deal with both estates on the same day.'

'Has the princess called you this afternoon?'

'Not yct. If she reads the paper, or if someone tells her the news, she will probably contact me. I still don't understand why my old friend was murdered. If it had happened anywhere but at his home, I would even swear that it was a case of mistaken identity.'

'I assume that Jaquette Larrieu was his mistress?'

'That isn't the word. Bear in mind that Saint-Hilaire never spoke of her to me. But I knew him. I knew Jaquette too, when she was young, and she was a very pretty girl. And yet Armand rarely let a pretty girl pass within range without trying his chances. He did it a little as an aesthete would, if you can understand that. Chances are, if the opportunity presented itself . . .'

'Jaquette had no family?'

'I wasn't aware of one. If she had brothers and sisters, it's a safe bet that they died a long time ago.'

'Thank you . . .'

'I assume you're in a hurry? Please know that I remain at your disposal. You too have the look of an honest man, and I hope you catch the rogue who has done this.'

Maigret still had the sense of being immersed in a past that had returned, a world that seemed to have vanished, and it was disconcerting to find himself back in the street, amidst the bustle of Paris, women shopping in tight trousers, bars with nickel-plated furniture, cars throbbing at the traffic lights.

He made for Rue Jacob, in vain, because on the door of the shop with the lowered shutters he found a black-edged sign announcing:

Closed due to bereavement.

He rang the bell several times without receiving an answer, then crossed to the other pavement to look at the first-floor windows. They were open, but there was not a sound to be heard. A woman with copper-coloured hair and a soft, full bosom emerged from the shadow of an art gallery.

'If it's about Monsieur Mazeron, he isn't at home. I saw him leaving at about midday after closing the shutters.'

She didn't know where he had gone.

'He's not very sociable . . .'

Maigret would visit Isabelle de V——, of course, but he was apprehensive about that visit and preferred to put it off until later, and to try to learn a little more about her first.

He had seldom been so perplexed by human beings. Would a psychiatrist, a teacher or a novelist, to quote the list in the *Lancet*, have been better placed to understand characters who had suddenly materialized from another century?

Only one thing was certain: Count Armand de Saint-Hilaire, a mild and inoffensive old man, and a man of honour, to use the notary's phrase, had been murdered, in his home, by someone he didn't suspect . . .

It was out of the question that it was an opportunistic, random crime, an anonymous and stupid one, first of all because nothing had disappeared, and then because the former ambassador was sitting peacefully at his desk when the first bullet, fired from close range, had struck him in the face.

Either he had gone to open the door to his visitor in person, or his visitor had a key to the apartment, even though Jaquette maintained that there were only two keys, hers and the count's.

Maigret, still rolling quite confused thoughts around in his head, went into a bar, ordered a beer and shut himself in the telephone cabin.

'Is that you, Moers? . . . Do you have the inventory in front of you? . . . Take a look and see if there's any mention of a key . . . The key to the door of the flat, yes . . . What? . . . Yes? Where did they find it? . . . In his trouser pocket? Thank you . . . No news? No . . . I'll go back to headquarters later on . . . If you have anything to tell me, call Janvier, who has stayed at Rue Saint-Dominique . . .'

They had found one of the two keys in the dead man's pocket, and Jaquette also had hers, because she had used it to open the door in the morning when Maigret and the man from the Foreign Ministry had followed her into the ground-floor flat.

People aren't killed without a motive. What was left, once theft had been ruled out? A crime of passion, among old people? A clash of interests?

Jaquette Larrieu was receiving a more than adequate lifelong pension, as the notary had informed him.

For his part, the nephew was inheriting the building and the bulk of the fortune.

As for Isabelle, it was hard to imagine that, with her husband only recently dead, the idea might have come to her . . .

No! No explanation was satisfactory, and the Foreign Ministry had categorically ruled out a political motive.

'Rue de la Pompe!' he said to the driver of a yellow taxi.

'Certainly, inspector.'

He had long since stopped being flattered at being recognized like that. The concierge sent him to the fifth floor, where a small and quite pretty brunette first half opened the door and then led Maigret into a sun-drenched flat.

'Excuse the chaos . . . I was making a dress for my daughter.'

She wore tight black silk trousers that clung to a well-rounded bottom.

'I expect you've come about the crime, and I wonder what you're hoping for from me.'

'Are your children not here?'

'My elder daughter is in England, to learn the language. She is living with a family as an au pair, and the younger one is working. It's for her that I'm . . .'

She pointed to a light, colourful piece of fabric on the table, from which she was cutting a dress.

'I assume you've seen my husband?'

'Yes.'

'How did he react?'

'How long is it since you last saw him?'

'Almost three years.'

'And the Count of Saint-Hilaire?'

'The last time he came up here was shortly before Christmas. He brought gifts for my daughters. He never forgot. Even when he was posted abroad and they were still quite small, he didn't forget Christmas and sent them a little something. That's how they ended up with dolls from all over the world. You can still see them in their bedroom.'

She was no more than forty and still very attractive.

'Is it true what the papers say? That he was murdered?'

'Tell me about your husband.'

Her face immediately hardened.

'What do you want me to tell you?'

'Was it a loving marriage? If I'm not mistaken, he's much older than you.'

'Only by ten years. He's never looked young.'

'Did you love him?'

'I don't know. I lived alone with my father, who was an

embittered person. He saw himself as a great misunderstood artist, and it pained him to have to earn his living by restoring pictures. I worked in a shop on the Grands Boulevards. I met Alain. Would you like something to drink?'

'No, thank you. I've just had a beer. Go on . . .'

'Perhaps I was attracted by his air of mystery. He wasn't like the others, he didn't speak much, and what he said was always interesting. We got married and immediately had a daughter.'

'You lived on Rue Jacob?'

'Yes. I liked that street too, and our little first-floor flat. At the time Saint-Hilaire was still an ambassador, in Washington if I remember correctly. He came to see us on leave once, then he had us to his house in Rue Saint-Dominique. I was very impressed by him.'

'What was his relationship with your husband?'

'I don't know how to put it. He was a man who seemed to treat everyone with kindness. He seemed surprised that I was his nephew's wife.'

'Why?'

'I didn't think I understood until much later, and even now I'm not sure. He must have known Alain better than I thought, better than I did at the time, at any rate . . .'

She broke off, as if worried by what she had just said.

'I don't want to give you the impression that I'm speaking like this out of rancour, because my husband and I are separated now. And in any case I was the one who left.'

'And no one tried to stop you?'

The furniture here was modern, the walls pale, and Maigret glimpsed a white and tidy kitchen. Familiar sounds rose from the street, while the greenery of the Bois de Boulogne spread out not far away.

'I assume you don't suspect Alain?'

'To be perfectly frank, I don't yet suspect anyone, but I wouldn't automatically rule out any possibility.'

'I'm sure you're barking up the wrong tree. In my view, Alain is an unhappy person who was never able to fit in and never will. Isn't it surprising that, leaving my father because he was an embittered man, I married a man even more embittered than he was? I only realized much later. In short, I have never seen him satisfied, and now I find myself wondering if he has ever smiled.

'He worries about everything, his health and his business, what people think about him, about the opinion of his neighbours and his clients . . .

'He thinks everyone is against him.

'It's hard to explain. Don't laugh at what I'm about to say. When I lived with him, I felt as if I could hear him thinking from dawn till dusk, an irritating stream of thought like the ticking of an alarm clock. He came and went in silence, suddenly looking at me as if his eyes had turned inwards, to a place that I was unable to reach. Is he still as pale as before?'

'He's pale, yes.'

'He already was when I met him and he remained so in the country, by the sea. An almost artificial pallor . . .

'And he never let anything show. There was no way of getting through to him . . . Over the years we slept in the same bed, and sometimes, when I woke up, I would look at him as if he was a stranger.

'He was cruel . . .'

She tried to find the right word.

'I'm probably exaggerating. He thought he was right, he wanted to be right at all costs. It was a mania of his. He was right down to the smallest details, and that's what made me speak of cruelty. I noticed it most of all when we had children. He looked at them the way he looked at me and others, with cold lucidity. If they did something silly, I tried to defend them.

' "At their age, Alain . . ."

' "There's no reason why they should get used to cheating."

'It was one of his favourite words. Cheating! Little acts of cheating! Little acts of cowardice!

'He brought that same intransigence into the tiniest details of daily live.

' "Why did you buy fish?"

'I was trying to explain that . . .

' "I said veal."

'When I went shopping . . .

'He would repeat, obstinately:

' "I said veal and you didn't need to go and buy fish." '

She broke off once more.

'Am I talking too much? I'm not saying stupid things?'

'Go on.'

'I've finished. After years, I thought I understood what the Americans understand by mental cruelty and why, over there, it has become a cause of divorce. There are teachers who, without raising their voices, rule over their classes with a kind of terror.

'With Alain my daughters and I were suffocating, and we didn't even have the consolation of seeing him going off to his office. He was downstairs, beneath our feet, from dawn till dusk, coming up ten times a day to study our actions and our movements with a frosty eye.

'I had to account for every franc I spent. And when I went out he demanded to know where I was going; he questioned me afterwards about the people I had spoken to, about what I had said and what they had replied . . .'

'Were you unfaithful to him?'

She wasn't outraged. It even seemed to Maigret that she was tempted to smile with a certain satisfaction, indeed a certain relish, but restrained herself.

'Why would you ask that? Have people talked to you about me?'

'No.'

'While I was living with him, I didn't do anything that he could reproach me for.'

'What made you decide to leave?'

'I had had enough. I was suffocating, as I say, and I wanted my daughters to grow up in a more breathable atmosphere.'

'You had no more personal reason for getting your freedom back?'

'Perhaps.'

'Did your daughters know?'

'I haven't hidden the fact that I have a boyfriend, and they're on my side.'

'Does he live with you?'

'I go and see him at his place. He's a widower, my age,

who was no happier with his wife than I was with my husband, so we both seem to be gluing the pieces back together.'

'Does he live around here?'

'In this very building, two floors down. He's a doctor. You'll see his plaque on the door. If Alain agrees to a divorce one day, we plan to marry, but I doubt it will happen. He is very Catholic, by tradition rather than conviction.'

'Does your husband make a living?'

'With ups and downs. When I left him, it was agreed that he would give me a modest maintenance for the children. He kept his word for a few months. Then there were delays. And in the end he stopped paying anything at all, on the grounds that they were old enough to earn a living. That still doesn't make him a murderer, does it?'

'Were you aware of his uncle's relationship?'

'You mean Isabelle?'

'Did you know that the Prince of V— died on Sunday morning, and that he was buried today?'

'I read it in the paper.'

'Do you think that if Saint-Hilaire had lived, he would have married the princess?'

'It's quite likely. He hoped for his whole life that they would be united one day. It touched me to hear him talking about her as if about an other-worldly being, an almost supernatural creature, when he was a man who appreciated the realities of life, sometimes even a little too much . . .'

This time she smiled openly.

'One day, a long time ago, when I went to see him, I

can't remember why, I had trouble keeping his hands off me. He wasn't embarrassed about it. In his eyes it was completely natural . . .'

'Did your husband know?'

She shrugged.

'Was he jealous?'

'In his way. We didn't have much contact, if you see what I mean, and it was always cold, almost mechanical. What he would have condemned wasn't that I might have been attracted to another man, but that I might be in error, I might commit a sin, a betrayal, an act that he considered somehow unclean. Forgive me if I've said too much, and if it sounds as if I'm blaming him, which isn't the case. You'll have noticed that I don't make myself sound any better than I am. It's a long time since I felt like a woman, and I'm making the most of it . . .'

She had a full mouth and sparkling eyes. For some minutes she had been crossing and uncrossing her legs.

'Are you sure I can't offer you something to drink?'

'Thank you. I should be off.'

'I assume this will all stay confidential?'

He smiled at her and walked towards the door, where she extended a chubby, warm hand.

'I'm going to get on with my daughter's dress,' she murmured, almost reluctantly.

So for a moment he had escaped the circle of old people. Leaving the flat on Rue de la Pompe, he wasn't surprised to find himself back in the street, with its noises and smells.

He immediately found a taxi and had it take him to Rue

Saint-Dominique. Before entering the building, he decided after all to have the beer that he had refused when it was offered by Madame Mazeron, and in the bar he rubbed shoulders with chauffeurs from the ministries and large firms.

The reporter was still there.

'As you see, I didn't try to follow you. I don't suppose you can tell me who you went to see?'

'The notary.'

'Did he tell you anything new?'

'Nothing.'

'Still no lead?'

'None.'

'Are we sure that it isn't political?'

'It would seem not to be.'

There was a uniformed policeman here too. Maigret rang the doorbell beside the lift shaft. Janvier opened the door in his shirt-sleeves; Jaquette wasn't in the office.

'What have you done with her? Did you let her go out?'

'No. She tried to, after the phone call, claiming that there was nothing to eat in the house.'

'Where is she?'

'In the bedroom. She's resting.'

'What phone call are you talking about?'

'Half an hour after you left, the phone rang, and I answered. I heard a woman's voice, quite faintly, at the end of the line.

'"Who is this?" she asked.

'Rather than replying, I asked in turn:

'"Who's calling?"

'"I would like to speak to Mademoiselle Larrieu."'

'"Who shall I say it is?"

'There was a silence, then:

'"The Princess of V—."

'Meanwhile Jaquette was watching me like someone who knew what was going on.

'"I'll just pass you to her."

'I held out the receiver and she said straight away:

'"It's me, your highness . . . yes . . . I would have liked to go, but these gentlemen won't let me leave the house . . . The apartment has been full of them, with all kinds of equipment . . . They spent hours asking me questions, and even now an inspector is listening to me . . ."'

Janvier added:

'She seemed to be defying me. After that she mostly listened.

'"Yes . . . Yes, your highness . . . yes . . . I understand . . . I don't know . . . No . . . Yes . . . I'll try . . . I'd like to do that too . . . Thank you, your highness . . ."'

'Then what did she say?'

'Nothing. She sat down on the chair again. After a quarter of an hour's silence she murmured regretfully:

'"I assume you aren't going to let me out? Even if there's nothing left to eat in the house and I have to go without supper?"

'"We'll sort that out shortly."

'"In that case I don't think there's much point us sitting here staring at each other, and I'd rather go and rest. Is that allowed?"

'Since then she's been in her bedroom. She's locked the door.'

'No one's come?'

'No. Some phone calls from an American press agency, some provincial papers . . .'

'You couldn't get anything out of Jaquette?'

'I've asked her some questions, as innocent as possible, in the hope of winning her trust. She merely said slyly:

'"Don't try and teach your grandmother to suck eggs, young man. If your boss imagined that I was going to reveal secrets to you . . ."'

'No one called from the office?'

'No. Only the examining magistrate.'

'Does he want to see me?'

'He asks you to call him as soon as you have any news. He had a visit from Alain Mazeron.'

'And you didn't tell me?'

'I was keeping that until last. So the nephew went to get him to complain that you read Saint-Hilaire's private correspondence without his permission. As an executor of the will, he requires that the flat be sealed until the reading of the will.'

'What did the judge say?'

'To talk to you.'

'And Mazeron didn't come back?'

'No. He might be on the way, because I received this communication not long ago. Do you think he'll come?'

Maigret hesitated and then pulled over a telephone directory, where he found what he was looking for, and then, standing up, looking serious and annoyed, he dialled a number.

'Hello! The V— residence? I would like to speak to

the Princess of V—. Detective Chief Inspector Maigret of the Police Judiciaire . . . I'll wait, yes . . .'

There was a different kind of silence in the room, and Janvier looked at his boss, holding his breath. A few minutes passed.

'No, I'm still here . . . Thank you . . . hello . . . Detective Chief Inspector Maigret, yes, madame . . .'

It wasn't his everyday voice, and he experienced the same feeling as he had done when, as a child, he addressed the Countess of Saint-Fiacre.

'I thought you might like me to contact you, if only to give you some details . . . Yes . . . Yes . . . Whenever you like . . . I'll be at Rue de Varenne in an hour . . .'

The two men looked at each other in silence. Finally, Maigret sighed.

'It would be better if you stayed here,' he said at last. 'Call Lucas and ask him to send someone. Ideally Lapointe. The old woman can go out whenever she likes, and one of the two of you will follow her.'

He had an hour ahead of him. While he waited, he took a bundle of letters out of the bookcase with the green curtain.

I saw you yesterday, at Longchamp, in your jacket, you know how much I love you like that. On your arm you had a pretty redhead who . . .

5.

Maigret didn't expect to find a house that still smelled like a funeral, like the houses of ordinary people and even the upper-middle classes, with odours of candles and chrysanthemums, a red-eyed widow, relatives who had come from far away, in full mourning, eating and drinking. Because of his country childhood, the smell of spirits, and particularly of marc, was still associated in his mind with death and funerals.

'Have a drop of this, Catherine,' they would say to the widow, before setting off for the church and the cemetery. 'You need picking up.'

She would drink, weeping. The men would drink at the inn, and then again back at the house.

If the entrance had been decorated with silver hangings that morning, they had been removed for a while now, and the courtyard had resumed its usual appearance, half in shade, half in sunlight, with a uniformed chauffeur washing a long black limousine and three automobiles, one a large sports car with yellow bodywork, waiting at the foot of the steps.

It was as huge as the Élysée Palace, and Maigret remembered that the V— residence was often the setting for balls and charity auctions.

At the top of the steps he pushed open the glass door

and found himself alone in a hall with marble tiles. Double doors, open on either side, allowed him to see the reception rooms where objects, probably the old coins and snuffboxes that had been mentioned to him, were exhibited as if in a museum.

Should he make for one of those doors, climb the double staircase that led to the first floor? He was hesitating when a butler, emerging from God knows where, approached in silence, took his hat from his hands and murmured, without asking him his name:

'This way.'

Maigret followed his guide along the stairs, passing through another drawing room on the first floor, and then a long room that must have been a picture gallery.

They didn't keep him waiting. The housekeeper half opened a door, announcing in a faint voice:

'Detective Chief Inspector Maigret.'

The boudoir that he entered overlooked not the courtyard of honour but a garden, and the foliage of the trees, full of birds, brushed against the two open windows.

Someone rose from an armchair, and it was a moment before he understood that it was the woman he had come to see, Princess Isabelle. His surprise must have been obvious, because she said as she came towards him:

'You weren't expecting to find me like this, were you?'

He didn't dare to reply that he wasn't. He was silent, surprised at first that, even though she was dressed in black, she didn't give the impression of being in full mourning, although he would have found it difficult to say why. Neither did she have red eyes. She didn't seem overwhelmed.

She was smaller than in her photographs, but unlike Jaquette, for example, the years didn't weigh heavy on her. He didn't have time to analyse his impressions. He would do it later. For now, he registered everything mechanically.

What surprised him the most was to find a plump woman, her cheeks full and smooth, with a round body. Her hips, barely perceptible in the princess dress in the photograph in Saint-Hilaire's bedroom, had become as broad as those of a farmer's wife.

Was the boudoir around them the room where she spent most of her time? Old tapestries decorated the walls. The parquet gleamed, each item of furniture in its place, and for no precise reason it reminded Maigret of the convent where as a child he had visited one of his aunts, who was a nun.

'Please, sit down.'

She pointed to a gilded armchair, but he chose instead a straight-backed chair, even though he was afraid of breaking its delicate legs.

'My first thought was to go there,' she confided in him, sitting down in turn, 'but I realized that he would have gone. The body has been taken to the Forensic Institute, hasn't it?'

She wasn't afraid of the words, or the images that they evoked. Her face was serene, almost smiling, and that too reminded him of the convent, the particular serenity of the sisters, who never seemed to be completely of this world.

'I would like to see him once more. I'll tell you about it

soon. What I need to know above all is whether he suffered. Tell me honestly.'

'Don't worry, madame. The Count of Saint-Hilaire was killed instantly.'

'Was he in his office?'

'Yes.'

'Sitting down?'

'Yes. Apparently he was busy correcting proofs.'

She closed her eyes, as if to give the image time to form in her mind, and Maigret was sufficiently emboldened to ask a question in turn.

'Have you ever been to Rue Saint-Dominique?'

'Only once, long ago, with Jaquette's complicity. I had chosen a time of day when I was sure he wasn't there. I wanted to get to know the setting of his life, to locate him in my mind at his home, in the different rooms.'

An idea struck her.

'I don't suppose you've read the letters?'

He hesitated for a moment and then chose to confess the truth.

'I ran through them. Not all of them, though.'

'Were they still in the Empire bookcase with the gilded grilles?'

He nodded.

'I suspected you would have read them. I don't blame you. I understand that it's your duty.'

'How did you learn of his death?'

'Through my daughter-in-law. Philippe, my son, came from Normandy with his wife and children for the funeral. Just now, on the way back from the cemetery, she flicked through one of the newspapers that the maidservants usually put on a table in the hall.'

'Is your daughter-in-law aware?'

She looked at him with a surprise that seemed almost naive. Had it been anyone else, he might have thought that she was playing a part.

'Aware of what?'

'Of your relationship with the Count of Saint-Hilaire.'

Her smile too was the smile of a nun.

'But of course. How could she not have been aware? We never hid ourselves. There was nothing bad between us. Armand was a very dear friend . . .'

'Did your son know him?'

'My son knew everything too, and when he was a child I sometimes pointed Armand out to him in the distance. I think the first time was in Auteuil . . .'

'He never went to see him?'

Her reply was not without logic, or at least it had a logic of her own:

'What for?'

Chirruping, the birds chased each other in the foliage, and an agreeable freshness came from the garden.

'Won't you have a cup of tea?'

Alain Mazeron's wife, in Rue de la Pompe, had offered him a drink. Here it was tea.

'No, thank you.'

'Tell me everything you know, Monsieur Maigret. You see, for fifty years I have become used to living with him in my thoughts. I knew what he was doing at every hour of the day. I visited the cities where he lived when he was still an ambassador and arranged with Jaquette to cast an eye over each of his houses in succession. At what time of day did he meet his death?'

'As far as we know, between eleven o'clock and midnight.'

'But he wasn't ready to go to bed.'

'How do you know?'

'Because before he went to his bedroom he always wrote me a little note that finished his daily letter. He began it every morning in a ritual fashion:

'"Good morning, Isi . . ."'

'As he would have welcomed me upon waking, if fate had allowed us to live together. He added a few lines and then, during the day, he came back to it to tell me what he had done. Invariably, in the evening, his last words were:

'"Goodnight, pretty Isi . . ."'

She smiled with confusion.

'Forgive me for repeating that word, which risks making you laugh. For him, I had stayed the twenty-year-old Isabelle.'

'He had seen you since.'

'In the distance, it's true. So he knew I had become an old woman, but for him the present was less real than the past. Can you understand that? He hadn't changed for me either. Now tell me what happened. Tell me everything, without trying to spare my feelings. When you reach my age, you see, you have a certain resilience. The murderer entered the apartment. Who? How?'

'Someone came in, because we haven't found a weapon either in the room or in the apartment. Since Jaquette maintains that she closed the door at about nine o'clock, as she does every evening, putting on the chain and bolt, we must believe that the Count of Saint-Hilaire welcomed his visitor himself. Do you know if he was in the habit of receiving people in the evening?'

'Never. Since his retirement he had followed a strict routine, and adopted a more or less invariable timetable. I could show you his letters from the last few years . . . You would see that the first phrases are often: "Good morning, Isi . . . I greet you, as I do every morning, because a new day is beginning, while I am beginning my monotonous little round . . ."'

'That was what he called his orderly days, which allowed no room for unpredictability.

'Unless I receive a letter by mail this evening . . . But no! It was Jaquette who posted them in the morning when she went to buy croissants. If she had put one in the box today, she would have told me on the phone . . .'

'What do you think of her?'

'She was very devoted to us, to Armand and me. When he broke his arm, in Switzerland, it was she who wrote to his dictation, and when later on he had an operation, she sent me a letter every day to keep me up to date.'

'You don't think she was jealous?'

She smiled again, and Maigret had trouble getting used to it. He was surprised by such calm and serenity, when he had expected a more or less dramatic exchange.

It was as if death didn't have the same meaning as it did elsewhere, as if Isabelle lived on equal terms with it, as if it were part of the normal course of life.

'She was jealous, but the way a dog is jealous of its master.'

He hesitated to ask certain questions, to approach certain subjects, and she was the one who put them on the table with disarming simplicity.

'If in the past she had been jealous in a different way, as a woman, it was of his mistresses, not of me.'

'Do you think she was his mistress too?'

'She certainly was.'

'Did he write to tell you?'

'He hid nothing from me, not even the humiliating things that men are reluctant to confide in their wives about. He wrote to me, for example, not many years ago:

'"Jaquette is nervous today. This evening I will have to give her her pleasure . . ."'

She seemed to be amused by Maigret's astonishment.

'Does that surprise you? And yet it's so natural.'

'You weren't jealous either?'

'Not of that. My only fear was that he would meet a woman who could take my place in his thoughts. Keep telling me what happened, inspector. Do we know nothing about his visitor?'

'Only that the first shot he fired was from a high-calibre weapon, probably a 7.65 automatic.'

'Where was Armand struck?'

'In the head. The pathologist says the death was instantaneous. The body slipped to the carpet, at the foot of the armchair. Then the murderer fired three more shots.'

'Why, if he was dead?'

'We don't know. Had the murderer gone mad? Was he

in a state of rage that made him lose his mind? It's hard to answer that question at this point. In the Court of Assizes, a murderer who tears in to his victim, who delivers a certain number of stab wounds, for example, is often accused of cruelty. And yet, on the basis of my experience and that of my colleagues, it is almost always the shy ones – I don't dare to say sensitive men – who act that way. They panic, they refuse to see their victims suffer and lose their heads . . .'

'Do you think that was the case?'

'Unless it's an act of revenge, of hatred bottled up for a long time, which is more unusual.'

He was starting to feel at ease with this old woman, who could say and hear anything.

'What would contradict this version is that it then occurred to the murderer to pick up the cartridge cases. They must have been scattered around the room, at a certain distance. He didn't miss a single one and he left no fingerprints. I still have one question, particularly after what you've told me about your relationship with Jaquette. After finding the body this morning, it doesn't seem to have occurred to her to call you, and she went not to the police station but to the Ministry of Foreign Affairs.'

'I think I can explain that. Immediately after my husband's death, the telephone started ringing almost without interruption. People we barely knew wanted information about the funeral, or to express their condolences to me. My son, exasperated, decided to disconnect the telephone.'

'So Jaquette might have tried to call you?'

'That's quite likely. And if she didn't come straight away to let me know, it was because she would have found it difficult to approach me on the day of the funeral.'

'Were you aware of the Count of Saint-Hilaire having any enemies?'

'Not at all.'

'In his letters, did he ever talk to you about his nephew?'

'Have you seen Alain?'

'This morning.'

'What does he say?'

'Nothing. He went to see Maître Aubonnet. The will is being read tomorrow, and the notary will have to contact you because your presence will be required.'

'I know.'

'Are you familiar with the terms of the will?'

'Armand planned to leave me his furniture and personal objects, so that if he passed away before me I would still have a sense of having been his wife.'

'Do you accept this legacy?'

'It's his will, isn't it? Mine too. If he hadn't died I would have become the Countess of Saint-Hilaire once my mourning was over. That was always agreed between us.'

'Was your husband aware of this plan?'

'Of course.'

'And your son and daughter-in-law?'

'Not just them, our friends as well. I repeat, we had nothing to hide. Now I'm going to be obliged, because of the name that I still bear, to live in this big house rather than move, as I have so often dreamed, to Rue Saint-Dominique. Armand's apartment will not be reconstructed here. I probably won't live for very long, but, little though it is, I will live in his surroundings as if I were his widow.'

Maigret was irritated by a phenomenon that was occurring within him. He found that he was fascinated by this woman, who was so different from everything he had known before. And not just by her, but by the legend that she and Saint-Hilaire had created, and in which they had lived.

At first glance it was as absurd as a fairy story or the instructive tales in children's books.

Here, in her presence, he was surprised to find himself believing in them. He adopted their way of seeing and feeling, rather in the way that at his aunt's convent he had walked on tiptoe and talked in a low voice, filled with unction and piety.

Then, all of a sudden, he saw her with another eye, the eye of the man from Quai des Orfèvres, and he was filled with revulsion.

Weren't they playing with him? Hadn't these people – Jaquette, Alain Mazeron, his wife with the tight trousers, Isabelle, and even Aubonnet, the notary – reached an agreement with each other?

There was a dead man, a real corpse with an open skull and a gaping belly. That assumed a murderer, and it wasn't just someone off the street who had entered the former ambassador's flat and killed him at close range before he could become suspicious and try to defend himself.

Over the years Maigret had learned that no one kills without a motive, without a serious motive. And even if in this instance the killer was a madman or a madwoman, they were a flesh-and-blood person who lived in the victim's circle.

Was Jaquette, with her aggressive suspicion, mad? Was Mazeron, whom his wife accused of mental cruelty, mad? Was it Isabelle who had lost some of her reason?

Every time he thought that way, he wanted to change tack and start asking cruel questions, if only to break through this suave exterior that they all adopted as if by contagion.

And every time he did, the princess disarmed and shamed him with a surprised, naive or even a mischievous expression.

'In short, you have no idea of the person who might have had an interest in killing Saint-Hilaire?'

'An interest, certainly not. You know as well as I do the broad lines of the will.'

'And if Alain Mazeron needed money?'

'His uncle gave him money when he needed it, and he would in any case have left him his fortune.'

'Did Mazeron know that?'

'I'm sure of it. Once my husband was dead, Armand and I would have married, it's true, but I wouldn't have allowed my family to inherit his property.'

'And Jaquette?'

'She was aware that her old age was taken care of.'

'And she was aware of your intention to go and live in Rue Saint-Dominique?'

'She was looking forward to it.'

Something within Maigret protested. All of this was false and inhuman.

'And your son?'

Surprised, she waited for him to clarify his point, and since Maigret remained silent she asked in turn:

'How is my son involved in this case?'

'I don't know. I'm searching. He is now the heir to the name.'

'He would have been even if Armand had lived.'

Obviously! But mightn't he have thought it a step down for his mother to marry Saint-Hilaire?

'Was your son here last night?'

'No. He stayed with his wife and children in a hotel on Place Vendôme, where they usually stay when they come to Paris.'

Maigret frowned and looked at the walls as if by staring through them he could measure the vastness of the building on the Rue de Varenne. Didn't it contain a considerable number of empty rooms, of unoccupied apartments?

'You mean that since he married he has never lived in this property?'

'First of all, he is seldom in Paris, and never for long, because he can't bear high society.'

'His wife too?'

'Yes. For the first years of their marriage they had an apartment in the house. And then they had one child, a second, a third . . .'

'How many do they have?'

'Six. The oldest is twenty, the youngest seven. This may shock you, but I can't live with children. It's a mistake to believe that all women are made to be mothers. I had Philippe because it was my duty. I looked after him as much as I had to. Years later, I couldn't have endured the sound of shouting and running about in the house. My son knows that. So does his wife.'

'They don't hold it against you?'

'They take me as I am, with my faults and foibles.'

'Were you alone here last night?'

'With the servants and two nuns keeping watch in the chapel of rest. Abbé Gauge, my spiritual adviser, who is also an old friend, stayed until ten o'clock.'

'You told me just now that your son and his family were in the house right now.'

'They are waiting to say goodbye to me, at least my daughter-in-law and the children. You must have seen their car in the courtyard. They are leaving for Normandy, apart from my son, who has to go with me to the notary tomorrow.'

'Would you allow me to have a brief conversation with your son?'

'Why not? I expected that question. I even thought that you would want to see the whole family, and that's why I asked my daughter-in-law to delay her departure.'

Was she being straightforward, or provocative? To return to the English doctor's theory, would a schoolteacher have been better at untangling the truth than Maigret?

He felt humbler than ever, more disarmed, amongst human beings whom he was attempting to judge.

'Come this way.'

She led him along the gallery and paused for a moment with her hand on the handle of a door, behind which voices could be heard.

She opened it and said simply:

'Detective Chief Inspector Maigret . . .'

And, in a huge room, the inspector saw first of all a child eating a cake, then a little girl of about ten asking her mother for something in a low voice.

Her mother was a tall blonde woman in her forties, with very pink skin, who looked like one of those robust Dutch-women that one sees in prints and postcards.

A thirteen-year-old boy was looking out of the window. The princess did her introductions, and Maigret registered the images one by one, with a view to reassembling them later like the pieces of a jigsaw.

'Frédéric, the oldest boy . . .'

A lanky young man, fair-haired like his mother, bowed slightly without holding out his hand.

'He too is destined for the diplomatic service.'

There was a daughter, a fifteen-year-old, and a boy of twelve or thirteen.

'Isn't Philippe here?'

'He went down to see if the car is ready.'

There was a sense of life suspended, as if in a station waiting room.

'Come this way, Monsieur Maigret.'

They followed another corridor, at the end of which they met a tall man, who watched them coming with a bored expression on his face.

'I was looking for you, Philippe. Inspector Maigret would like to talk to you for a moment. Where would you like to receive him?'

Philippe held out his hand, apparently somewhat distracted, but curious enough to see a policeman at close quarters.

'Anywhere. Here.'

He pushed open a door leading into an office with red hangings, in which portraits of ancestors hung on the walls.

'I will leave you, Monsieur Maigret, asking you to keep me informed. As soon as the body is brought back to Rue Saint-Dominique, be kind enough to let me know.'

She disappeared, light and insubstantial.

'You wanted to talk to me?'

Whose office was it? Probably nobody's, because there was nothing to indicate that anyone had ever worked there. Philippe de V— pointed to a chair and held out his cigarette case.

'No, thank you.'

'You don't smoke?'

'Only a pipe.'

'Me too, usually. But not in this house. My mother hates it.'

There was a kind of ennui, or perhaps impatience, in his voice.

'I assume you want to talk to me about Saint-Hilaire?'

'You know he was murdered last night?'

'My wife told me just now. It's a curious coincidence, admit it.'

'You mean that his death might have had some connection with your father's?'

'I don't know. The papers are silent on the circumstances of the crime. I assume suicide is out of the question?'

'Why would you ask that? Did the count have reasons to kill himself?'

'I can't think of any, but you never know what's going on in people's heads.'

'Did you know him?'

'My mother pointed him out to me when I was a child. I sometimes bumped into him later on.'

'Did you talk to him?'

'Never.'

'Were you angry with him?'

'Why would I have been?'

The man seemed honestly surprised by the questions he was being asked. He too had the appearance of an honest man who had nothing to hide.

'Throughout her life my mother devoted a kind of mystical love to him that never gave us reason to be ashamed. Besides, my father was the first to smile about it with a hint of tenderness.'

'When did you get back from Normandy?'

'Sunday afternoon. I had come on my own last week, after my father's accident, and then left again, because he seemed to be in fine fettle. I was surprised on Sunday when my mother called me to say that he had died of an attack of uraemia.'

'Did you travel with your family?'

'No. My wife and children didn't arrive until Monday. Except for my eldest son, of course, who is at the École Normale Supérieure.'

'Did your mother talk to you about Saint-Hilaire?'

'What do you mean?'

'Perhaps my question is ridiculous. Did she say at any point that she might marry the count?'

'She didn't need to talk to me about it. I had been aware for a long time that if my father died before she did, that marriage would take place.'

'You never shared your father's society lifestyle?'

He seemed surprised by all of this and reflected before answering.

'I think I understand your point of view. You have seen photographs of my father and mother in magazines, when they went to some foreign court, or when they attended a grand wedding or a princely engagement party. Obviously I also attended some of these events when I was between eighteen and twenty-five. Let's say twenty-five, more or less. After that I got married and went to live in the country. Have they told you that I graduated from Grignon agricultural college? My father gave me one of his properties, in Normandy, and we live there as a family. Is that what you wanted to know?'

'You have no suspicions?'

'About the murderer of Saint-Hilaire?'

It seemed to Maigret that the man's lip was trembling slightly, but he couldn't have sworn.

'No. Not what one could really call a suspicion.'

'But you have had an idea?'

'It wouldn't stand up, and I would rather not talk about it.'

'Were you thinking about someone whose life would be changed by your father's death?'

Philippe de V—, whose eyes had been lowered for a moment, looked up.

'Let's say that it's passed through my mind, but I didn't linger over it. I've heard so much about Jaquette and her devotion . . .'

He seemed uneasy about the whole conversation.

'I don't want to rush you. I have to say goodbye to my family and I would like them to be home before nightfall.'

'Will you stay in Paris for a few more days?'

'Until tomorrow night.'

'Place Vendôme?'

'My mother told you that?'

'Yes. To put my conscience at ease, I would like to ask you one more question and request that you don't take umbrage. I was obliged to ask your mother too.'

'Where I was last night, I assume? At what time?'

'Let's say between ten in the evening and midnight?'

'That's quite a long time. Wait! I had dinner here with my mother.'

'Alone with her?'

'Yes. I left at about nine thirty after the arrival of Abbé Gauge, whom I'm not fond of. I went back to the hotel to kiss my wife and children goodnight.'

A silence. Philippe de V— looked straight ahead, hesitant and embarrassed.

'Then I took the air on the Champs-Élysées . . .'

'Until midnight?'

'No.'

This time he looked Maigret in the eyes, with a slightly shameful smile.

'It might seem strange to you, given my very recent bereavement. It's a sort of tradition for me. At Genestoux I'm too well known to allow myself any kind of romantic adventure, and it would never even occur to me. Is it because of my childhood memories? Every time I come to Paris, I have the habit of spending an hour or two with a pretty woman. Since I insist that it goes no further, and doesn't complicate my life, I merely . . .'

He waved his hand vaguely.

'On the Champs-Élysées?' Maigret asked.

'I wouldn't say it in front of my wife, who wouldn't understand. For her, outside of a certain world . . .'

'What's your wife's maiden name?'

'Irène de Marchangy . . . I might clarify, if it's of any use to you, that my companion of yesterday is a brunette, not very tall, that she was wearing a pale-green dress and has a beauty spot under her breast. I think it's the left breast but I'm not sure.'

'Did you go to hers?'

'I assume she lives in the hotel on Rue de Berry that she took me to, because there were clothes in the wardrobe and personal objects in the bathroom.'

Maigret smiled.

'I'm sorry to rush you, and thank you for your patience. Has that removed any doubts you might have had about me? This way! I'll let you go down on your own, because I'm in a hurry to . . .'

He looked at his watch and held out his hand.

'Let me wish you good luck!'

In the main courtyard, a chauffeur was waiting by a limousine whose engine was running with a barely audible hum.

Five minutes later, Maigret literally dived into the thick atmosphere of a bistro and ordered a beer.

6.

He was woken by the sun coming in through the slats of the shutters and, with a movement that had become mechanical after so many years, reached towards his wife's side of the bed. The sheets were still warm. Along with the smell of freshly ground coffee, a faint whistle reached him from the kitchen, the sound of water singing in the kettle.

Here too, as in the aristocratic Rue de Varenne, birds chirped in the trees, less close to the windows, and Maigret felt a sense of physical well-being, albeit mingled with something vague and unpleasant.

He had slept fitfully. He remembered having lots of dreams and even, at least once, waking with a start.

At a certain point, hadn't his wife whispered something to him, holding out a glass of water?

It was difficult to remember. Several different stories had become confused, and he kept losing the thread. They had one thing in common: in all of them, he played a humiliating role.

One picture came back to him, clearer than the others: a place that looked like the V— residence, but much larger, if less opulent. It was like a convent or ministerial offices, with endless corridors and an infinity of doors.

What he had just done was not clear in his mind. He

only knew that he had a goal to reach, and that it was enormously important. And yet he couldn't find anyone to tell him the way. Pardon had told him as they parted in the street. He didn't see Dr Pardon in his dream, or in the street. He was no less certain that his friend had warned him.

The truth was that he wasn't allowed to ask the way. He had tried to at the beginning, before understanding that it was impossible. The old people merely looked at him, smiling and shaking their heads.

Because there were old people everywhere. Perhaps it was a retirement home, or an asylum, even though it didn't look like one.

He recognized Saint-Hilaire, very straight-backed, his face pink beneath his silky white hair. A very handsome man, who knew it and seemed to be making fun of the inspector. Maître Aubonnet was sitting in a wheelchair and amusing himself by racing it very quickly along a gallery.

There were many others, including the Prince of V—, with a hand on Isabelle's shoulder, indulgently observing Maigret's efforts.

The inspector's situation was delicate, because he had not yet been initiated, and they were refusing to tell him what tests he had to pass.

He was in the position of a new recruit, a new boy at school. They played tricks on him. For example, every time he tried to open a door it closed by itself or, rather than opening on to a bedroom or a drawing room, it revealed the start of a new corridor.

Only the old Countess of Saint-Fiacre was willing to help him. Since she wasn't allowed to speak, she tried to communicate to him with gestures, which didn't work. For example, she pointed to her own knees, and, lowering his eyes, Maigret discovered that he was in short trousers.

Madame Maigret, in the kitchen, was at last pouring water on the coffee. Maigret opened his eyes, frowning at the memory of this stupid dream. All in all, it was as if he had been trying to enter a circle, which happened to be the circle of old people. And if they hadn't taken him seriously, it was because they saw him as a little boy.

Even sitting on his bed, he was still perplexed, vaguely watching after his wife, who had just set a cup of coffee down on his bedside table and was now opening the shutters.

'You shouldn't have eaten snails last night . . .'

To distract himself after a disappointing day, he had taken her to dinner at a restaurant and eaten snails.

'How do you feel?'

'Fine.'

He wasn't going to let a dream spoil his day. He drank his coffee, went into the dining room and glanced at the newspaper as he had his breakfast.

It contained a few more details than the previous day's report on the death of Armand de Saint-Hilaire, and they had found quite a good photograph of him. There was one of Jaquette as well, caught as she was entering a dairy. It was when she had gone to do her shopping with Lapointe on her heels the previous evening.

Quai d'Orsay is categorically ruling out the suggestion of a political crime. On the other hand, well-informed circles are connecting the death of the count with another, accidental death which happened three days ago.

That meant that the story of Saint-Hilaire and Isabelle would be told at length in a future edition.

Maigret still felt sluggish and lacklustre, and it was at such moments that he regretted not choosing another profession.

He waited for the bus at Place Voltaire and was lucky enough to find one with a platform where he could smoke his pipe while watching the streets passing by. At Quai des Orfèvres he greeted the office boy with a wave of his hand, climbed the stairs, which a cleaning woman was sweeping after scattering a few drops of water to stop the dust from blowing away.

On his desk he found a large pile of documents, reports and photographs.

The photographs of the dead man were shocking. Some of them showed his whole body, as he had been found, with a leg of the desk in the foreground and stains on the carpet. There were also photographs of his head, his chest, his belly, when he was still dressed.

Other numbered shots indicated the entry point of each bullet and a dark bulge under the skin, on the back, where one of the bullets had stopped after breaking the collarbone.

There was a knock at the door, and a very fresh-looking Lucas appeared, clean shaven and with talcum under his ear.

'Dupeu is here, chief.'

'Show him in.'

Inspector Dupeu, like Isabelle's son, had a large family, six or seven children, but it was not out of a sense of irony that Maigret had entrusted him with a certain mission the previous day. He had just happened to be available at the right moment.

'So?'

'The prince's account is quite accurate. I went to Rue de Berry at about ten o'clock in the evening. As usual, there were four or five girls on the street. Among them there was only one little brunette, who told me that she hadn't been there the previous day because she had gone to see her baby in the country.

'I waited for quite a long time and saw another one coming out of a hotel with an American soldier.

'"Why are you asking?" she said anxiously when I put my question. "Are the police after him?"

'"Not at all. It's just a check."

'"Tall, about fifty, quite well built?"'

Dupeu went on:

'I asked the girl if she had a beauty spot under her breast, and she said she did, and she had another one on her hip. Of course the man didn't say his name, but on the evening of the day before yesterday she only went with him because he offered her three times the price that she normally asks.

'"And yet he only stayed for half an hour . . ."

'"At what time did he approach you?"

'"At ten to eleven. I remember because I was coming

out of the bar next door, where I had gone for a coffee, and I looked at the clock behind the counter."'

Maigret observed:

'If he only spent half an hour with her, that means he left her before half past eleven?'

'That's what she said.'

Isabelle's son hadn't lied. No one in this case seemed to be lying. It was true that if he left Rue de Berry at half past eleven he could easily have been at Rue Saint-Dominique before midnight.

Why would he have gone to his mother's old lover? And more importantly, why kill him?

The inspector had had no more luck with the nephew, Alain Mazeron. The previous day, just before dinner, Maigret had called in at Rue Jacob and found nobody at home. Then he had phoned at about eight o'clock and had no reply.

After that he had told Lucas to send somebody to the antique shop early in the morning. It was Bonfils, who came to the office in turn with equally disappointing information.

'He wasn't even slightly troubled by my questions.'

'Was his shop open?'

'No. I had to ring. He looked through the first-floor window before coming down, unshaven, in braces. I asked him how he had spent his time the previous afternoon and evening. He told me that he had gone to see the notary first of all.'

'That's true.'

'I'm sure. Then he went to Rue Drouot, where there

was an auction of helmets, uniform buttons and weapons from the Napoleonic era. He claims that some collectors are avid for these relics. He bought a lot and showed me a pink piece of paper detailing the objects that he has to collect this morning.'

'And then?'

'He went for dinner in a restaurant in Rue de Seine, where he almost always has his meals. I've checked.'

Another one who hadn't lied! A strange job, Maigret thought, when you're disappointed that someone hasn't killed a person! That was the case, and the inspector, in spite of himself, was annoyed with these people for being innocent or seeming as if they were.

Because, in spite of everything, there was a corpse.

He picked up his phone.

'Will you come down, Moers?'

He didn't believe in the perfect crime. In twenty-five years with the Police Judiciaire, he hadn't come across such a thing. Certainly, he could remember some crimes that had gone unpunished. Often you knew the guilty man, who had had time to skip abroad. Either that or they were poisonings or crimes motived by financial gain.

That wasn't the case this time. A random low-life wouldn't have got into the flat on Rue Saint-Dominique, fired four bullets at an old man sitting at his desk then left again without taking anything.

'Come in, Moers. Sit down.'

'Have you read my report?'

'Not yet.'

Maigret didn't admit that he hadn't felt up to reading

it, any more than he had the eighteen pages from the pathologist. The previous day he had given Moers and his men the task of looking for physical clues, and he trusted them, knowing very well that nothing would escape them.

'Has Gastinne-Renette sent his conclusions?'

'They are in the file. It's a 7.65 automatic pistol, either a Browning or one of the many imitations that you can buy.'

'Are we sure that there wasn't a single cartridge case in the apartment?'

'My men have searched every square centimetre.'

'No weapon either?'

'No weapon, no ammunition apart from hunting rifles and their cartridges.'

'Any fingerprints?'

'The ones from the previous day, the count's prints and those of the concierge's wife. I took them by chance before leaving Rue Saint-Dominique. The concierge's wife came twice a week to help Jaquette Larrieu clean the flat from top to bottom.'

Moers looked embarrassed and uneasy.

'I've included the inventory of objects found in the drawers and cupboards. But I went over the place for much of the night without discovering anything strange or unexpected.'

'Any money?'

'A few thousand francs in a wallet, some change in a kitchen drawer and, in the office, some chequebooks from the Rothschild Bank.'

'Any cheque stubs?'

'Cheque stubs too. The poor old man was so far from expecting to die that he ordered a suit ten days ago from a tailor on Boulevard Haussmann.'

'No prints on the window-sill?'

'Nothing.'

They only needed to look at each other to understand. They had worked together for years and had trouble remembering a single case when, going over the scene of the crime with a fine-tooth comb, as the papers say, they didn't discover some detail that was anomalous, at least at first sight.

Here, everything was too perfect. Everything had a logical explanation, everything except the old man's death.

By wiping the butt of the gun and putting it in the man's hand, the killer could have tried to make it look like suicide. Obviously provided that he had only fired the first bullet. But why fire three more?

And why couldn't they trace the former ambassador's automatic? He had possessed one, that much was clear. Old Jaquette confessed that she had seen it a few months before, in the chest of drawers in the bedroom.

The gun was no longer in the flat, and according to the maidservant's account it was more or less the size and weight of a 7.65 pistol.

Presumably the former ambassador had allowed someone in . . . Someone he knew, because he had gone back to sit at his desk, in his dressing gown . . .

In front of him, a bottle of cognac and a glass . . . Why hadn't he offered his visitor a drink?

How had the scene played out? That visitor walking towards the bedroom – along the corridor or through the dining room – picking up the pistol, coming into the office, walking up to the count and firing a first shot at point-blank range . . .

'It doesn't add up . . .' Maigret sighed.

He also needed a motive, a motive compelling enough for the perpetrator to risk a death sentence.

'I assume you didn't subject Jaquette to the paraffin test?'

'I wouldn't have dared without first talking to you.'

When a firearm is used, particularly a pistol with automatic ejection, the explosion sends out particles which embed themselves in the gunman's skin, particularly on the edge of the hand, and remain there for a period of time.

Maigret had thought of that the previous day. But did he have the right to suspect the old housekeeper any more than anyone else?

Admittedly she was the one best placed to have committed the crime. She knew where to find the gun, she could move around the flat while her employer was working without provoking his suspicion, she could walk over to him and fire, and it was quite possible that while the body lay on the carpet she might have continued to pull the trigger.

She was so meticulous that she might then have looked around the room for cartridge cases.

But was it possible that she would, after that, have gone peacefully to bed, a few metres away from her victim?

That in the morning, on her way to Quai d'Orsay, she would have stopped somewhere, on the banks of the Seine, for example, or on the Pont de la Concorde, to get rid of the gun and the cartridge cases?

She had a motive, or something like one. For almost fifty years she had lived with Saint-Hilaire, in his shadow. He concealed nothing from her, and it appeared highly likely that they had had intimate relations in the past.

The ambassador didn't seem to attach much importance to that, and neither did Isabelle, who smiled as she spoke of it.

But what about Jaquette? Was she not the old man's true companion?

She knew of his platonic love of the princess, she posted his daily letters, and it was she who had once shown Isabelle into the flat when her master was out.

'I wonder if . . .'

Maigret was repelled by the hypothesis, which seemed too easy. While he was able to conceive of it, he didn't *feel* it.

Once the Prince of V— was dead and Isabelle was free, the old lovers would finally be able to marry. They had only to wait for the end of the mourning period to go to the city hall and the church and they would live together in Rue Saint-Dominique or Rue de Varenne.

'Listen, Moers . . . I'm going to ask you to go over there. Be nice to Jaquette. Don't frighten her. Tell her it's only a formality . . .'

'Shall I try the test?'

'It would put my mind at rest.'

When he was told a little later that Monsieur Cromières was on the line, he asked his colleagues to say he was out and they didn't know when he would be back.

The reading of the Prince of V—'s will was due that morning. Isabelle and her son would shortly find themselves in the presence of the old notary Aubonnet, and the princess would come back later on for the reading of another will.

The two men in her life, on the same day . . .

He called Rue Saint-Dominique. The previous day he had been reluctant to seal the doors of the office and the bedroom. Instead he had chosen to wait, or to keep open the option of revisiting the scene.

Lapointe, whom he had left on guard duty, had probably been sleeping in an armchair.

'Is that you, chief?'

'No news?'

'Nothing.'

'Where is Jaquette?'

'At six o'clock this morning, when I was keeping watch in the office, I heard her walking along the corridor, dragging a vacuum cleaner behind her. I hurried to ask her what she was planning to do and she looked at me in astonishment.

'"Cleaning, of course!"

'"Cleaning what?"

'"First the bedroom, then the dining room, then . . ."'

Maigret muttered:

'Did you let her?'

'No. She didn't seem to understand why.

'"What am I going to do, then?" she asked me.'

'What did you reply?'

'I asked her to make me some coffee, and she went off to buy croissants.'

'Could she have stopped on the way to make a phone call or post a letter?'

'No. I told the policeman watching the door to follow her from a distance. She really did just go into the bakery and she only stayed there for a moment.'

'Is she angry?'

'It's hard to tell. She walks around moving her lips, as if talking to herself. Right now she's in the kitchen, and I don't know what she's doing.'

'Have there been any phone calls?'

The French windows to the garden must have been open because Maigret could hear the twittering of blackbirds coming down the line.

'Moers will join you in a few minutes. He's already on his way. Are you tired?'

'I must confess that I've been asleep.'

'I'll have someone take over from you soon.'

An idea came into his head.

'Don't hang up. Go and ask Jaquette to show you her gloves.'

She was a regular church-goer, and he was sure that she would wear gloves for Sunday mass.

'I'll stay on the line.'

He waited, holding the receiver. Quite a long time passed.

'Are you there, chief?'

'Well?'

'She showed me three pairs.'

'Wasn't she surprised?'

'She glared at me before going and opening a drawer in her bedroom. I spotted a missal, two or three rosaries, postcards, medals, handkerchiefs and gloves. Two pairs are in white cotton.'

Maigret could see her in the summer, with white gloves and, probably, a touch of white in her hat.

'And the other pair?'

'Black suede, quite worn.'

'I'll see you later.'

Maigret's question had to do with Moers' mission. Saint-Hilaire's murderer could have learned from the newspapers that powder is embedded in a gunman's hands a certain length of time after firing. If Jaquette had used the gun, mightn't it have occurred to her to put on some gloves? And in that case, wouldn't she have got rid of them?

To be clear in his own mind, Maigret immersed himself in the file that was still spread out in front of him. He found the inventory with the contents of each item of furniture, listed piece by piece.

Maid's room . . . An iron bedstead . . . An old mahogany table covered with a fringed square of crimson velvet . . .

His finger followed the typed lines:

Eleven handkerchiefs, six of them marked with the initial J . . . Three pairs of gloves . . .

She had shown the three pairs to Lapointe.

He left without taking his hat and walked to the door that connected the Police Judiciaire with the Palais de Justice. He had never paid a visit to the examining magistrate Urbain de Chézaud, who had previously been in Versailles, and with whom he had never had the opportunity to work before. He had to go to the third floor, where the oldest offices were, and at last found the magistrate's visiting card on a door.

'Come in, Monsieur Maigret. I am very pleased to see you, and I was in fact wondering if I shouldn't call you.'

He was in his forties and intelligent-looking. On his desk Maigret recognized the copy of the file that he had received himself, and noticed that some of the pages were already annotated in red pencil.

'We haven't got many physical clues, have we?' the judge sighed, inviting Maigret to sit down. 'I've just had a call from the Foreign Ministry . . .'

'Young Monsieur Cromières . . .'

'He claims he's been trying in vain to get in touch with you and wonders where the morning papers got their information.'

The clerk behind Maigret was typing. The windows overlooked the courtyard, and it seemed likely that these people never saw the sun.

'Have you any news?'

Because he liked the magistrate, Maigret didn't hide his discouragement.

'You've read . . .' he sighed, pointing at the file. 'I'll give you a preliminary report tonight or tomorrow. Theft wasn't the motive for the crime. Neither does it seem to have been inspired by financial interests, because that would be too obvious. The victim's nephew is the only one who benefits from Saint-Hilaire's death. And it would only gain him a few months, or a few years.'

'Does he have pressing financial concerns?'

'Yes and no. It's hard to extract a firm response from these people without baldly accusing them. And I have no basis for an accusation. Mazeron lives apart from his wife and daughters. He is a cold and rather disagreeable character, and his wife describes him as a kind of sadist.

'Looking at his antique shop, it seems as if no one ever goes in. It's true that he specializes in military trophies, and there are a few passionate devotees of such objects.

'He sometimes asked his uncle for money. There's nothing to indicate that he didn't give it with good grace.

'Was he worried that once Saint-Hilaire was married he might lose his inheritance? It's possible. I don't think so. Those families have a particular mentality. Each of them considers himself as the depository of property that he has the duty to pass on, more or less intact, to his direct or indirect descendants.'

He caught a smile on the magistrate's lips and remembered that he was called Urbain de Chézaud, another aristocratic name.

'Go on.'

'I met Madame Mazeron, in her flat in Passy, and I'm struggling to think why she would have gone to kill her husband's uncle. I'll say the same of their two daughters. Besides, one of them is in England. The other is working.'

Maigret stuffed his pipe.

'May I?'

'Please do. I smoke a pipe as well.'

It was the first time he had found himself face to face with a pipe-smoking magistrate. The latter added:

'At home, in the evening, when I'm studying my dossiers.'

'I went to see Princess of V—.'

He looked at the magistrate.

'You are aware of her history, aren't you?'

Maigret was sure that Urbain de Chézaud moved in circles where people were interested in Isabelle.

'I've heard of it.'

'Is it true that her relationship with the count, if we can call it a relationship, is well known to many people?'

'In certain circles, yes. Her friends call her Isi.'

'That's what the count calls her in his letters as well.'

'Have you read them?'

'Not all of them. Not every word. There are enough to fill several volumes. It seemed to me, but it's only an impression, that the princess wasn't as devastated by Saint-Hilaire's death as might have been expected.'

'In my view nothing in life has ever been able to strip her of her serenity. I met her occasionally. I've heard friends talking about her. It sounds as if she never got beyond a certain age, and time stopped for her. Some claim she stopped at twenty, others that she hasn't changed since convent school.'

'The papers are telling her story. They've started to allude to it.'

'I've seen. It was inevitable.'

'When I questioned her, she didn't tell me anything that gave me a hint of a lead. This morning she's gone to see the notary about her husband's will. She'll be back in the afternoon for Saint-Hilaire's.'

'Does she stand to inherit?'

'Only the furniture and the personal effects.'

'Have you seen her son?'

'Philippe, his wife and their children. They were all together at Rue de Varenne. Only the son stayed in Paris.'

'What do you make of them?'

Maigret was obliged to reply:

'I don't know.'

Strictly speaking, Philippe too had a reason to kill Saint-Hilaire. He was about to become heir to the historic line of V—, related to all the courts of Europe.

His father had come to terms with Isabelle's platonic love of the discreet ambassador, whom she only saw from a distance, and to whom she sent childlike letters.

Now that he was dead, the situation would change. Even though she was seventy-two and her lover was seventy-seven, the princess was going to marry Saint-Hilaire, lose her title, change her name.

Was that a good enough motive for a crime and – Maigret kept coming back to this – to risk the death penalty? In short, to replace a fairly anodyne scandal with a much more serious one?

The inspector murmured, embarrassed:

'I've checked what he got up to on Tuesday evening. He stayed in a hotel on Place Vendôme with his family, as he always does. Once the children were in bed he went out on his own and walked up the Champs-Élysées. On the corner of Rue de Berry, he chose from the five or six girls who were available and followed one of them home.'

Maigret had often seen murderers, *after* their crimes, chasing after a woman, any woman, as if they felt the need to relax.

He couldn't remember a single one acting that way *beforehand*. To get himself an alibi?

In that case, the alibi wasn't complete, because Philippe de V— had left the girl at about 11.30, giving himself time to go to Rue Saint-Dominique.

'That's as far as I've got. I'm going to go on looking for another lead, although I don't expect to find one, perhaps someone else who was close to the former ambassador, and whom no one has yet mentioned. Saint-Hilaire had regular habits, as most old men do. Almost all his friends are dead . . .'

The phone rang. The clerk got up to answer it.

'Yes . . . He's right here . . . Do you want me to pass him to you?'

And, turning towards the inspector:

'It's for you. Apparently it's very urgent.'

'May I?'

'Please do.'

'Hello! . . . Maigret, yes . . . Who's speaking?'

He didn't recognize the voice because Moers, who eventually gave his name, was over excited.

'I tried to reach you at your office. I was told that—'

'What is it?'

'I'm getting there. It's so extraordinary! I've just finished the test—'

'I know. And?'

'It's positive.'

'Are you sure?'

'Absolutely. There is no doubt that Jaquette Larrieu fired one shot or several within the last forty-eight hours.'

'She agreed to the test?'

'Quite readily.'

'What explanation has she given?'

'None. I haven't said anything to her. I had to go back to the lab to finish the test.'

'Is Lapointe still with her?'

'He was there when I left Rue Saint-Dominique.'

'Are you sure of your claim?'

'I'm certain.'

'Thank you.'

He hung up, with a serious expression, a wrinkle in the middle of his forehead, under the questioning gaze of the examining magistrate.

'I was wrong,' Maigret murmured regretfully.

'What do you mean?'

'Quite at random, without believing it, I admit, I asked the lab to try the paraffin test on Jaquette's right hand.'

'And it's positive? That's what I thought I understood, but I found it hard to believe.'

'Me too.'

He should have felt as if a great weight had been lifted from him. So, after barely twenty-four hours of investigation, the problem that had seemed insoluble to him a moment earlier had been solved.

And yet it gave him no satisfaction.

'While I'm here, would you sign me a warrant?' he sighed.

'You're going to send your men to arrest her?'

'I'll go myself.'

And Maigret dejectedly relit his pipe, while the magistrate silently filled in the blanks of a printed form.

7.

Maigret called in at his office to pick up his hat. Just as he was leaving he had a sudden anxiety and, cross with himself for not having thought of it sooner, dashed to the telephone.

To gain some time, he dialled the number of Rue Saint-Dominique without going through the switchboard. He was anxious to hear Lapointe's voice and check that nothing had happened over there. Instead of a ring tone, he heard the intermittent hum of the engaged signal.

He couldn't think straight and lost his composure for a few seconds.

Who would Lapointe have had reason to call? Moers had left him a short time before. Lapointe knew he would immediately contact the inspector to deliver his report.

If the inspector left in Saint-Hilaire's flat was on the phone, it meant that something unexpected had happened, and he was calling the Police Judiciaire or maybe a doctor.

Maigret opened the door of the nearby office and saw Janvier lighting a cigarette.

'Go down and wait for me in the courtyard at the wheel of a car.'

He made one last attempt to call, and heard the same buzzing noise at the other end.

A short time later he could be seen running down the stairs, getting into the little black car in a hurry and slamming the door.

The car raced towards Pont Saint-Michel and turned right along the river, while cars pulled over and passers-by stopped to watch it go by.

Maigret might have been overreacting, but he couldn't dispel the image of a dead Jaquette, and Lapointe, nearby, hanging on the telephone. It became so real in his mind that he tried to work out how Jaquette had taken her life. She couldn't have thrown herself out of the window, because the flat was on the ground floor. She had no weapon at her disposal except the kitchen knives.

The car stopped. The policeman at his post near the coach-gate, in full sunlight, was surprised by the siren. The bedroom window was half open.

Maigret ran towards the entrance, climbed the stone steps, pressed the electric doorbell and immediately found himself face to face with Lapointe, who was both calm and baffled.

'What's going on, chief?'

'Where is she?'

'In her bedroom.'

'When did you last hear her moving about?'

'Just now.'

'Who were you phoning?'

'I was trying to reach you.'

'Why?'

'She's getting dressed as if to go out, and I wanted to ask your instructions.'

Maigret felt ridiculous in front of young Lapointe, and Janvier, who had just joined them. In contrast with the anxiety of the last few minutes, the flat was calmer than ever; he found the office bathed in sunlight, the door open on to the garden, the lime tree twittering with birds.

He went back into the kitchen, where everything was tidy, and heard faint sounds in the old housekeeper's bedroom.

'Can I see you, Mademoiselle Larrieu?'

He had once called her *madame*, and she had protested, saying:

'*Mademoiselle*, if you please!'

'Who is it?'

'Inspector Maigret.'

'I'll be right there.'

Lapointe went on in a low voice:

'She had a bath in her master's bathroom.'

Maigret had seldom been so dissatisfied with himself, and he remembered his dream, the old people looking at him condescendingly and shaking their heads because he was in short trousers and they saw him only as a small boy.

The door of the little bedroom opened, and a breath of perfume reached him, a perfume that had long been out of fashion, and which he recognized because his mother wore it on Sundays to go to high mass.

And high mass was what Jaquette seemed to be dressed for. She wore a black silk dress, a starched black kerchief around her neck, a black hat decorated with white faille and immaculate gloves. The only thing missing was the missal in her hand.

'I am obliged,' he murmured, 'to take you to Quai des Orfèvres.'

He was about to display the arrest warrant signed by the judge, but, contrary to his expectations, she did not appear to be either surprised or indignant. Without a word, she passed through the kitchen, where she checked that the gas had been turned off, and went into the office to shut the door and pull the French windows closed.

She asked only one question.

'Is anyone going to stay here?'

And, since she did not receive an answer straight away, she added:

'If not, the bedroom window should be closed.'

Not only, even knowing that she had been discovered, did she have no intention of killing herself, she had never been so dignified, so self-controlled. She was the first to leave. Maigret said to Lapointe:

'You should stay.'

She walked ahead, nodding faintly to the concierge, who was watching her through the glass door.

Wouldn't it have been ridiculous, hateful, to put handcuffs on this woman of almost seventy-five? Maigret invited her to get into the car and sat down beside her.

'You don't need the siren now.'

The weather was still glorious, and they overtook a big red-and-white coach full of foreign tourists. Maigret couldn't think of anything to say, any questions to ask.

Hundreds of times he had gone back to Quai des Orfèvres like this with a suspect, male or female, whom he would have to force into a corner. His task was more or less difficult, more or less awkward according to the case. It could go on for hours, and sometimes the interrogation wouldn't end until daybreak, when the ordinary people of Paris began to go to work.

For Maigret, this phase of an inquiry was always disagreeable.

For the first time, he was going to perform the operation on an old woman.

In the courtyard of the Police Judiciaire, he helped her out of the car, and she waved away the hand he extended, walking with dignity towards the staircase, as if crossing the square in front of a church. He gestured to Janvier to join them. All three of them climbed the big staircase and reached the inspector's office, where the breeze swelled the curtains.

'Please, sit down.'

Even though she had been shown to an armchair, she chose an ordinary chair, while Janvier, who knew the routine, sat down at one end of the desk, picking up a pad and a pencil.

Maigret coughed a little, stuffed a pipe and walked to the window, then came back to stand in front of the old woman, who looked at him with motionless, keen little eyes.

'Before we do anything else, I must tell you that the examining magistrate has just signed a warrant for your arrest.'

He showed it to her. She gave the document only polite attention.

'You are accused of the deliberate homicide of your employer, Count Armand de Saint-Hilaire, during the night of Tuesday to Wednesday. An expert from the forensic department has recently carried out a paraffin test on your right hand. This test consists of collecting the fragments of powder and chemicals that have become embedded in the skin of a person when they use a firearm, particularly an automatic ejecting pistol.'

He watched her, hoping for a reaction, and she was the one who seemed to be studying him, she was the calmer of the two, the more in control of herself.

'You're not saying anything?'

'I have nothing to say.'

'The test was positive, which establishes beyond any possible error that you recently used a firearm.'

Quite impassive, she could just as easily have been in church listening to the sermon.

'What did you do with that weapon? I imagine that on Wednesday morning you went to Quai d'Orsay and threw it into the Seine along with the cartridge cases? I should warn you that every means necessary will be employed to recover the pistol, that divers will go down to the river bed.'

She had decided to say nothing and she said nothing. Her expression remained so serene that one might have thought she was not the focus of attention, that she was there by chance, witnessing a conversation that had nothing to do with her.

'I don't know what your motive might have been, although I have my suspicions. You lived for almost fifty years with the Count of Saint-Hilaire. You were as intimate with him as two people can be.'

A very faint smile hovered around Jaquette's lips, a smile that contained both coquettishness and a profound feeling of satisfaction.

'You knew that, after the death of the prince, your employer would make his youthful dream come true.'

It was irritating, like talking to a brick wall, and from time to time Maigret had to stop himself from shaking the old woman by the shoulders.

'If he hadn't died, he would have got married. Is that what you think? Would you have kept your position in the house? And if you had, would that position have been exactly the same?'

Pencil in the air, Janvier was still waiting for a reply to record.

'On Tuesday evening you went into the count's office. He was revising the proofs of his book. Did you have a conversation with him?'

Another ten minutes of questions without answers, and Maigret, exasperated, felt the need to go and unwind in the inspectors' office. It reminded him that Lapointe had been at Rue Saint-Dominique since the previous evening.

'Are you busy, Lucas?'

'Nothing urgent.'

'Go and take over from Lapointe.'

Then, because it was after midday, he added:

'Drop in at the Brasserie Dauphine. Have them send up a tray of sandwiches, some beer and some coffee.'

And, thinking of the old woman:

'A bottle of mineral water as well.'

In his office, he found Jaquette and Janvier still sitting motionless in their places as if in a painting.

For half an hour he paced the room, puffing on his pipe, stopping at the window and standing a few steps away from the housekeeper to look her in the eyes.

It wasn't an interrogation, because she remained stubbornly silent, but a long and more or less disconnected monologue.

'It's possible, I can tell you straight away, that experts will concede diminished responsibility. Your lawyer will certainly argue for a crime of passion . . .'

It seemed ridiculous, but it was true.

'It's not in your interest to remain silent, while by pleading guilty you have every chance of moving the jury. Why not start now?'

Children play this kind of game: it's about not opening your mouth whatever your partner says and does, and particularly not laughing.

Jaquette wasn't speaking or laughing. She watched Maigret's every move, still as if it had nothing to do with her, without flinching, without refusal.

'The count was the only man in your life.'

What was the point? He was trying in vain to find the tender spot. There was a knock on the door. It was the waiter from the Brasserie Dauphine, who set the tray down on Maigret's desk.

'It would do you good to eat something. At the rate we're going, we're likely to be here for some time.'

He held out a ham sandwich to her. The waiter had

gone. She lifted a corner of the white bread and, by a miracle, opened her mouth at last.

'It's over fifteen years since I last ate meat. Old people don't need it.'

'Would you rather have some cheese?'

'I'm not hungry anyway.'

He went back to the inspectors' office.

'Phone down to the brasserie for some cheese sandwiches.'

He ate while walking, as if taking his revenge, his pipe in one hand, his sandwich in the other, and every now and again he stopped to take a sip of beer. Janvier had abandoned his pencil to eat as well.

'Would you rather talk to me with no one else present?'

He received only a shrug.

'You have the right to have a lawyer of your choice present. I'm ready to call whoever you suggest. Do you know a lawyer?'

'No.'

'Would you like me to give you the list?'

'There's no point.'

'Would you rather I appointed a duty solicitor?'

'That won't help.'

They were making progress, because she had opened her lips.

'You admit you shot your employer?'

'I have nothing to say.'

'In other words, you have sworn to remain silent, whatever happens?'

That exasperating silence fell again. Pipe smoke floated in the office, with the sunlight coming in from one side. The air began to smell of ham, beer and coffee.

'Would you like a cup of coffee?'

'I only drink coffee in the morning, with a lot of milk.'

'What do you want to drink?'

'Nothing.'

'Do you plan to go on hunger strike?'

That was a mistake, because she smiled at the idea, perhaps even finding it appealing.

He had seen suspects of all kinds here, in similar circumstances, hard men and softies, some who wept or who turned more and more pale, others who defied or mocked him.

It was the first time that anyone sitting on that chair had shown such indifference and calm obstinacy.

'You still don't want to say anything?'

'Not now.'

'When do you think you will speak?'

'I don't know.'

'Are you waiting for something?'

Silence.

'Do you want me to call the Princess of V—?'

She shook her head.

'Is there anyone you would like to send a message to, or anyone you would like to see?'

Cheese sandwiches were brought, which she looked at with indifference. She shook her head and said over and over again:

'Not now.'

'So you've made up your mind not to talk, not to drink, not to eat.'

Her chair was uncomfortable, and almost everyone who had sat on it had soon felt ill at ease. After an hour she was still sitting just as straight, without moving her feet or her arms, without having changed position.

'Listen, Jaquette . . .'

She frowned, shocked by this familiarity, and it was the inspector who was embarrassed.

'I should warn you that we will stay in this room for as long as necessary. We have the physical proof that you fired at least one shot. I am just asking you to tell me why and in what circumstances. With your stupid silence . . .'

The word had slipped out, and he started over again.

'With your silence, you risk misleading the police, and putting suspicion on other people. If in half an hour you haven't answered my questions, I will ask the princess to come here and put her in your presence. I will also summon her son, and Alain Mazeron and his wife, and we will see if this general confrontation . . .'

He shouted angrily:

'What is it?'

There had been a knock at the door. Old Joseph pulled him into the corridor and whispered, with his head lowered:

'There's a young man who insists—'

'What young man?'

Joseph held out a visiting card in the name of Julien de V—, Isabelle's grandson.

'Where is he?'

'In the waiting room. He says he's in a hurry because he has an important class that he can't miss.'

'Keep him waiting for a moment.'

He came back into the office.

'Isabelle's grandson, Julien, is asking to see me. He has something to say to me. Are you still planning to keep your mouth shut?'

It was certainly exasperating, but it was also pathetic. Maigret saw that the old woman was in a state of inner conflict and he was reluctant to press her. Janvier himself, who was only an onlooker, seemed to be struggling with his conscience.

'You'll have to speak eventually. So why don't you . . .'

'Am I allowed to see a priest?'

'Do you want to confess?'

'I'm just asking permission to talk to a priest for a few minutes, Abbé Barraud.'

'Where can I reach Abbé Barraud?'

'At the presbytery of Sainte-Clotilde.'

'Is he your spiritual adviser?'

He didn't want to let the slightest chance go and picked up the phone.

'Put me through to the presbytery of the parish of Sainte-Clotilde . . . Yes . . . I'll stay on the line. Abbé Barraud . . . It doesn't matter how it's spelt . . .'

He rearranged the pipes on his desk, and lined them up in single file like lead soldiers.

'Hello . . . Abbé Barraud? . . . This is the Police Judiciaire . . . Maigret, detective chief inspector . . . I have in my office one of your parishioners who wants to talk to you . . . Yes, it's Mademoiselle Larrieu . . . Can you take a taxi to Quai des Orfèvres? . . . Thank you . . . Yes, she's waiting for you.'

And, to Janvier:

'When the priest gets here, bring him in and leave them on their own together . . . There's someone I have to see in the meantime.'

He made for the glazed waiting room, where there was no one but the young man in black he had seen the previous day on Rue de Varenne with his parents and his brothers and sisters. At the sight of Maigret he got up and followed the inspector into a little empty office.

'Take a seat.'

'I haven't got long. I have to go back to Rue d'Ulm, where I have a class in half an hour.'

In the tiny room he looked taller and lankier. The expression on his face was serious and slightly sad.

'I almost spoke to you yesterday, when you came to see my grandmother.'

Why did Maigret find himself thinking that he would have liked to have a son like this boy? He had a natural ease as well as a kind of innate modesty, and if he seemed a little withdrawn, one had a sense that it was only out of delicacy.

'I don't know if what I have to say will be of any use to you. I thought a lot about it last night. On Tuesday afternoon I went to see my uncle.'

'Your uncle?'

The young man blushed, a faint redness that disappeared again immediately, making way for a shy smile.

'That's what I called the Count of Saint-Hilaire.'

'Did you spend time with him?'

'Yes. I talked to my parents about it. I didn't hide it either. Even when I was very small I'd heard people talking about him.'

'Who?'

'My governesses first of all, then later my fellow pupils. My grandmother's love story is almost legendary.'

'I know.'

'At the age of ten or eleven I asked her about it, and we used to talk about Saint-Hilaire together. She read me certain letters, the ones in which he talked about diplomatic receptions, for example, conversations with heads of state. Have you read his letters?'

'No.'

'He wrote very well, with great vivacity, a bit like Cardinal de Retz. Perhaps it's because of the count and his stories that I chose a career in the diplomatic service.'

'When did you meet him in person?'

'Two years ago. I had a classmate at Stanislas whose grandfather was also in the diplomatic service. One day at his house I met the Count of Saint-Hilaire and asked to be introduced to him. I thought I could feel his emotion as he examined me from head to toe, and I was quite moved too. He asked questions about my studies, my plans.'

'Did you go and see him at Rue Saint-Dominique?'

'He had invited me there, although he added:

'"As long as your parents don't think it awkward."'

'Did you visit him often?'

'No. About once a month. It depended. For example, I

asked his advice after my baccalaureate, and he encouraged me in my plan to go to the École Normale. He too thought that, even if it didn't help my career, it would still give me a solid foundation.

'One day I said without thinking:

'"I sometimes have a sense that I'm confiding in my uncle."

'"And I in a nephew," he answered with a laugh. "Why don't you call me 'uncle'?"

'That explains the word that slipped out just now.'

'Didn't you like your grandfather?'

'I didn't know him very well. While he and the Count of Saint-Hilaire might have belonged to the same generation, they were very different men. For me my grandfather was always an imposing and inaccessible figure.'

'And your grandmother?'

'We were great friends. We still are.'

'Was she aware of your visits to Rue Saint-Dominique?'

'Yes. I reported our conversations back to her. She demanded details and, sometimes, she was the one who reminded me that I hadn't been to see our friend for a long time.'

Maigret, drawn though he was to the young man, was nonetheless studying him with amazement, almost with suspicion. Meeting young people of this kind is a rare occurrence at Quai des Orfèvres, and once again he had the sensation of an unreal universe, of people who had come not from life but from the pages of an edifying book.

'So on Tuesday afternoon you went to Rue Saint-Dominique.'

'Yes.'

'Did you have any particular reason to pay this visit?'

'More or less. My grandfather had died two days before. I thought my grandmother would like to know what her friend's reaction was.'

'Didn't you have the same curiosity?'

'Perhaps I did. I knew they had sworn they would marry if they had the chance one day.'

'And you were charmed by that prospect?'

'To some extent, yes.'

'And your parents?'

'I never talked about it to my father, but I have every reason to think that he wouldn't mind. My mother, perhaps . . . ?'

As he didn't finish his sentence. Maigret insisted:

'Your mother . . . ?'

'I'm not being mean about her if I say that she attaches more importance to titles and privilege than the rest of the family.'

Probably because she wasn't born a princess, but plain Irène de Marchangy.

'What happened during that conversation at Rue Saint-Dominique?'

'Nothing that I can clearly explain. Nonetheless, I thought it was better to talk to you about it. The Count of Saint-Hilaire seemed concerned at first, and I suddenly saw that he was very old. Before, he was a man who didn't look his age. One had a sense that he loved life, that he savoured every aspect, every moment. In my eyes he was a character who had strayed from the eighteenth century into our own. Do you understand what I mean?'

Maigret nodded.

'I didn't expect to see him seriously affected by the death of my grandfather, who was two years his senior, particularly since the death was accidental, and we knew that my grandfather had barely suffered. And yet on Tuesday afternoon, Saint-Hilaire was downcast and avoided my eye as if he was hiding something from me.

'I said something like:

'"In a year you will marry my grandmother at last . . ."

'As he turned his head away, I pressed the point:

'"Does that trouble you?"

'I wish I could remember his exact words. It's strange that I can't, given that I was so struck by their meaning and all that they implied.

'Essentially he replied:

'"They won't let me."

'And when I looked at his face, I thought I read fear in it.

'You see, it's all quite vague. At the time I didn't attach too much importance to it, thinking that it was the natural reaction of an old man learning of the death of another old man and thinking that it would soon be his turn.

'When I learned that he had been murdered, that scene came back to me.'

'Did you talk to anyone about it?'

'No.'

'Not even your grandmother?'

'I didn't want to bother her. I would swear, in

retrospect, that the count felt threatened. He wasn't the kind of man to worry about nothing. In spite of his age he was still exceptionally lucid, and his philosophy sheltered him against unjustified worries.'

'If I understand correctly, you think he predicted what happened to him.'

'He predicted a misfortune, yes. I preferred to come and talk to you because it's been bothering me since yesterday.'

'Did he ever talk to you about his friends?'

'About his dead friends, yes. He had no living friends left, but that didn't affect him unduly.

'"All in all," he said, "it isn't disagreeable to be the very last one."

'He added in a melancholy voice:

'"There's always a memory in which the others go on living."'

'He didn't talk to you about his enemies?'

'I'm sure he never had any. Perhaps some people who were jealous at the start of his career, when he was a rising star. They're in the cemetery too.'

'Thank you. You did the right thing in coming.'

'You still don't know anything?'

Maigret hesitated and almost mentioned Jaquette, who at that very moment must have been shut away in his office with Abbé Barraud.

Sometimes at police headquarters they called Maigret's office 'the confessional', and yet this was the first time that it had really served that purpose.

'Nothing definite, no.'

'I need to get back to Rue d'Ulm.'

Maigret led him to the top of the stairs.

'Thanks again.'

For a moment he paced the huge corridor, his hands behind his back, then lit his pipe and went into the inspectors' office. Janvier was there, apparently waiting.

'Is the priest next door?'

'He has been for some time.'

'What's he like?'

And Janvier replied with slightly bitter irony:

'He's the oldest of the lot!'

8.

'Call Lucas.'

'Rue Saint-Dominique?'

'Yes. I sent him to take over from Lapointe.'

He was starting to get impatient. The murmur of conversation continued in the adjacent office, and when they approached the door they could only hear a whisper, as if they were outside a real confessional.

'Lucas? . . . Everything quiet over there? . . . Only phone calls from journalists? . . . Keep telling them there's no news . . . What? . . . No! She hasn't spoken . . . She's in my office, yes, but not with me, or any of our men . . . With a priest . . .'

A moment later it was the examining magistrate on the end of the line, and Maigret repeated more or less the same words.

'I'm not being rough with her, no, don't worry. Quite the contrary . . .'

He couldn't remember being so gentle, so patient in his life. The article that Pardon had read to him came back to his memory and made him smile ironically.

The contributor to the *Lancet* had been mistaken. It wasn't a teacher, at the end of the day, or a novelist, nor even a policeman who would solve Jaquette's problem, but an octogenarian priest.

'How long have they been in there?'

'Twenty-five minutes.'

He didn't have the consolation of a glass of beer, because the tray was still in the next room. Soon it would be lukewarm. If it wasn't already. He was tempted to go down to the Brasserie Dauphine, but reluctant to leave at that moment.

He felt that the solution was near at hand and tried to guess what it was, less as an inspector with the Police Judiciaire who had been entrusted with the task of catching a criminal and persuading him to confess, than as a man.

Because it was as a man that he had conducted this investigation, as a personal matter, so much so that he had mixed in his own childhood memories.

Wasn't he slightly involved himself? If Saint-Hilaire had been ambassador for several decades, if his and Isabelle's platonic affair dated back almost fifty years, he, Maigret, had twenty-five years in the Police Judiciaire behind him, and as recently as the previous day he had been convinced that he had seen every possible category of human being pass in front of him.

He didn't consider himself as superhuman, he didn't think he was infallible. On the contrary, he began his investigations with a certain humility, even the simplest ones.

He was suspicious of evidence, of hasty judgements. He patiently tried to understand, bearing in mind that the most obvious motives are not always the deepest.

While he might not have a lofty notion of men and their possibilities, he still believed in mankind.

He looked for weak points. And when at last he put his finger on them, he didn't celebrate his victory but on the contrary felt a certain despondency.

He had lost his confidence since the previous day, unprepared in the face of people whose existence he hadn't even suspected. All their attitudes, their ideas, their reactions were alien to him, and he tried in vain to classify them under any particular category.

He wanted to like them, even Jaquette, who was driving him mad.

He found in their lives a grace and harmony, a certain naivety that charmed him.

All of a sudden he said to himself coldly:

'Saint-Hilaire still got killed.'

By one of them, it was almost certain. By Jaquette, if the scientific tests meant anything at all.

For a few moments he took a sudden dislike to them all, including the dead man, including that young man who had made him feel more strongly than ever a longing for fatherhood.

Why couldn't they have been like other people? Why couldn't they have had the same sordid interests and the same passions?

All of a sudden he was exasperated by that overly innocent love story. He stopped thinking about it and looked for something else, a different explanation, one that conformed more fully to his experience.

Surely two women who have loved the same man for many years must end up hating each other?

Doesn't a family related to most of the crowned families

of Europe react to the threat of a marriage as ridiculous as the union envisaged by the two old people?

None of them levelled accusations. None of them had any enemies. They all lived together in apparent harmony, except Alain Mazeron and his wife, who had ended up separating.

Irritated by the endless whispering, Maigret was close to violently opening the door, and what stopped him was perhaps the reproachful look that Janvier darted at him.

He too was charmed!

'I hope you're keeping an eye on the corridor?'

He was almost considering the possibility of the old priest making off with his penitent.

And yet he felt that he was close to touching the truth that escaped him. It was very simple, he knew. Human tragedies are always simple when we reconsider them in retrospect. Several times since the previous day, and particularly since this morning, he couldn't have said exactly when he had been on the brink of understanding.

Some discreet knocks on the communicating door made him jump.

'Shall I come with you?' Janvier asked.

'That would be better.'

Abbé Barraud was standing there, very old, in fact, and skeletal, with very long, wild hair in a halo around his skull. His cassock was shiny and worn, and had been badly mended in places.

Jaquette seemed not to have left the chair, where she was still sitting as straight as before. Only the expression on her face had changed. It was no longer tense, it had given up struggling. It no longer expressed defiance, or the fierce determination to remain silent.

While she wasn't smiling, she still radiated serenity.

'Forgive me, inspector, for keeping you waiting so long. You see, the question that Mademoiselle Larrieu asked me was quite delicate, and I had to consider it seriously before giving it an answer. I confess that I almost asked your permission to telephone the Monseigneur to ask his advice.'

Janvier, seated at the end of the table, was taking the discussion down in shorthand. Maigret, as if he needed to regain his composure, had sat down at his desk.

'Have a seat, reverend.'

'Are you letting me stay?'

'I should imagine your penitent still needs your services?'

The priest sat down on a chair, brought out a box-wood case from his cassock and took a pinch of snuff. This action, and the grains of tobacco on the greyish cassock, brought old memories back to Maigret.

'Mademoiselle Larrieu, as you know, is very devout, and her piety dictated an attitude which I thought it my duty to make her abandon. Her concern was that the Count of Saint-Hilaire would not be allowed a Christian burial, and that was why she decided to wait until the funeral had taken place before she spoke.'

For Maigret it was like a child's balloon suddenly bursting in the sun, and he blushed to have been so close to the truth without reaching the end.

'The Count of Saint-Hilaire committed suicide?'

'Unfortunately that's the truth. As I said to Mademoiselle Larrieu, there is no proof that he didn't repent of his action at the very last moment. No death is instantaneous in the eyes of the Church. Infinity exists in time as it does in space, and an infinitely small period of time, beyond the measurement of doctors, is enough for contrition.

'I don't believe the Church would refuse the Count of Saint-Hilaire its final blessing.'

For the first time Jaquette's eyes darkened, and she took a handkerchief from her bag to wipe them, while a girlish pout appeared on her lips.

'Speak, Jaquette,' the priest said encouragingly. 'Repeat what you told me.'

She swallowed her saliva.

'I had gone to bed. I was asleep. I heard a report and dashed to the office.'

'You found your master stretched out on the carpet, with half his face blown away.'

'Yes.'

'Where was the pistol?'

'On the desk.'

'What did you do?'

'I went to my bedroom to fetch a mirror to check that he had stopped breathing.'

'So you checked that he was dead. And then?'

'My first idea was to telephone the princess.'

'Why didn't you?'

'First of all because it was almost midnight.'

'You weren't afraid that she would disapprove of your plan?'

'I didn't think about it straight away. I said to myself that the police were going to come, and all of a sudden I thought that because of the suicide the count would have a civil burial.'

'How long passed between the moment when you knew the count was dead and the moment when you fired in your turn?'

'I don't know. Perhaps ten minutes? I knelt down beside him and prayed. Then, standing up, I grabbed the pistol and fired it, without looking, asking forgiveness of both the dead man and heaven.'

'You fired three bullets?'

'I don't know. I pulled the trigger until it stopped working. Then I noticed some gleaming dots on the carpet. It's not something I know about. I worked out that they were the cartridge cases and I picked them up. I didn't sleep that night. Early in the morning I went to throw the gun and the cartridge cases in the Seine, from Pont de la Concorde. I must have waited for a certain amount of time, because there was a policeman posted outside the Chamber of Deputies who seemed to be looking at me.'

'Do you know why your boss killed himself?'

She looked at the priest, who gave her a sign of encouragement. 'He had been anxious and discouraged for a while.'

'For what reason?'

'A few months ago, the doctor had advised him to stop drinking wine and spirits. He loved wine. He did without it for several days, then began to drink it again. That gave him stomach pains, and he had to get up at night to take bicarbonate of soda. In the end I was buying him a packet every week.'

'What's the name of his doctor?'

'Dr Ourgaud.'

Maigret picked up the receiver.

'Put me through to Dr Ourgaud, please.'

And to Jaquette:

'Had he been his doctor for a long time?'

'For ever, you might say.'

'How old is Dr Ourgaud?'

'I don't know exactly. More or less my age.'

'And he still practises?'

'He sees his old patients. His son is in the same surgery, on Boulevard Saint-Germain.'

Right up until the end they stayed not only in the same neighbourhood, but among people of the same kind.

'Hello! Dr Ourgaud? Inspector Maigret here.'

He was asked to speak louder and closer to the receiver, and the doctor apologized for being a little hard of hearing.

'As you suspect, I would like to ask you some questions about one of your patients. Yes, it's about him, Jaquette Larrieu is in my office and she has just told me that the Count of Saint-Hilaire committed suicide . . . What? . . . You were waiting for me to pay you a visit? The idea had occurred to you? . . . Hello! I'm speaking as close to the receiver as possible . . . She claims that for a few months the Count of Saint-Hilaire had suffered from stomach pains . . . I can hear you perfectly . . . Dr Tudelle, the pathologist who carried out the post-mortem, said he was surprised to find an old man's organs in such good condition . . .

'What? . . . That's what you kept telling your patient? He didn't believe you?

'Thank you, doctor. I will probably be obliged to disturb you to take your statement . . . Absolutely not! It's very important, on the contrary . . .'

He hung up with a serious expression, and Janvier thought he seemed moved.

'The Count of Saint-Hilaire', he explained in quite a bleak voice, 'had got it into his head that he was suffering from cancer. In spite of the reassuring words of his physician, he began to have himself examined by other doctors and was convinced each time that they were hiding the truth from him.'

Jaquette murmured:

'He had always been so proud of his health! He often repeated to me, in the old days, that he wasn't afraid of death, that he was prepared for it, but that he would find it hard to bear living with a disability. When he had flu, for example, he hid away like a sick animal and tried to keep me out of his room as much as possible. That was his vanity. A few years ago, one of his friends died of a cancer that had kept him in bed for almost two years. He was made to undergo complicated treatments, and the count said impatiently, "Why don't they just let him die? If I was in his place, I'd ask them to help me to go as soon as possible."'

Isabelle's grandson, Julien, didn't remember the exact words that Saint-Hilaire had uttered a few hours before dying. Thinking he would be happy to see his dream close to realization, he had had before him a worried and anxious old man, who seemed to be afraid of something.

That, at least, was what Julien had believed, because he himself wasn't yet an old man. Jaquette had understood straight away. And Maigret, who was halfway there, closer to the old people than to students in the Rue d'Ulm, understood as well: Saint-Hilaire expected, any day, to be bedbound.

And he expected that to happen just as an old love that nothing had tarnished for fifty years was on the point of becoming real life.

Isabelle, who saw him only in the distance, and who had retained in her mind the image of their youth, would become a caregiver at the same time as she became a wife, and would know only the miseries of an exhausted body.

'Will you excuse me?' he said suddenly, heading for the door.

He reached the corridors of the Palais de Justice, climbed to the third floor and spent half an hour locked away with the examining magistrate.

When he came back to his office, the three figures were still in the same place, and Janvier was chewing on his pencil.

'You are free,' he told Jaquette. 'We'll have you driven back. Or rather, I think I should have you driven to Aubonnet, the notary, where you have an appointment. As to you, Monsieur l'Abbé, we will have you dropped off at the presbytery. Over the next few days there will be some formalities to accomplish, some papers to sign.'

And, turning to Janvier:

'Do you want to take the wheel?'

He spent an hour with the commissioner of the Police Judiciaire, and he was then seen in the Brasserie Dauphine, where he had two large glasses of beer at the counter.

Madame Maigret must have been expecting him to call and tell her that he wouldn't be coming home for dinner, as so often happened in the course of an investigation.

She was surprised, at 6.30, to hear his footsteps on the stairs and she opened the door just as he reached the landing.

He was more serious than usual, with a serene seriousness, but she didn't dare to question him when, as he kissed her, he held her to him for a long time without saying a word.

She couldn't have known that he had just been immersed in a distant past, and a future that was a little less distant.

'What's for dinner?' he asked at last, as if rousing himself.

OTHER TITLES IN THE SERIES

MAIGRET TRAVELS
GEORGES SIMENON

'*Eyes half-closed, head tilted against the back of his seat, he seemed not to be thinking, as the plane flew over a thick carpet of bright clouds. In reality, he was making an effort to bring names and shadowy figures to life, names and figures that even this morning had been as unknown to him as the inhabitants of another planet.*'

The attempted suicide of a countess and the death of a billionaire in the same luxury Paris hotel send Maigret to the Riviera and then to Switzerland, as he searches for the truth amid the glittering world of the super-rich.

Translated by Howard Curtis

OTHER TITLES IN THE SERIES

MAIGRET'S DOUBTS
GEORGES SIMENON

'At this time the previous day he had never heard of the Martons, the train-set specialist was beginning to haunt his thoughts, and so was the elegant young woman who, he admitted, had boldly stood up to him when he had done everything he could to unsettle her.'

When a salesman from a Paris department store confides his secret fears to Maigret, the Inspector soon becomes caught up in a treacherous feud between husband and wife that is not as clear cut as it seems.

Translated by Shaun Whiteside

OTHER TITLES IN THE SERIES

MAIGRET AND THE RELUCTANT WITNESSES
GEORGES SIMENON

'It was as if suddenly, long ago, life had stopped here, not the life of the man lying on the bed but the life of the house, the life of its world, and even the factory chimney that could be seen through the curtains looked obsolete and absurd.'

A once-wealthy family closes ranks when one of their own is shot, leaving Maigret – along with a troublesome new magistrate – to pick his way through their secrets.

Translated by William Hobson

OTHER TITLES IN THE SERIES

MAIGRET'S SECRET
GEORGES SIMENON

'*Certain details of the case were etched more sharply than others in Maigret's memory. Even years later he could recall the particular taste and smell of the rain shower in Rue Caulaincourt as keenly as a childhood memory.*'

At a dinner party one evening, Maigret tells the story of an old case – the trial and execution of a man who may have been innocent – and how it has haunted him ever since.

Translated by David Watson

INSPECTOR MAIGRET

OTHER TITLES IN THE SERIES

MAIGRET IN COURT
GEORGES SIMENON

'They suddenly found themselves in an impersonal world, where everyday words no longer seemed to mean anything, where the most mundane details were translated into unintelligible formulae. The judges' black gowns, the ermine, the prosecutor's red robe further added to the impression of a ceremony set in stone where the individual counted for nothing.'

When Maigret is called to testify in court and reveals his doubts about a picture-framer accused of double murder, his actions have tragic consequences that he could never have foreseen.

Translated by Ros Schwartz

OTHER TITLES IN THE SERIES